A CANDLELIGHT ROMANCE

CANDLELIGHT ROMANCES

214 Pandora's Box, BETTY HALE HYATT
215 Safe Harbor, JENNIFER BLAIR
216 A Gift of Violets, JANETTE RADCLIFFE
217 Stranger on the Beach, ARLENE HALE
218 To Last a Lifetime, JENNIFER BLAIR
219 The Way to the Heart, GAIL EVERETT
220 Nurse in Residence, ARLENE HALE
221 The Raven Sisters, DOROTHY MACK
222 When Dreams Come True, ARLENE HALE
223 When Summer Ends, GAIL EVERETT
224 Love's Surprise, GAIL EVERETT
225 The Substitute Bride, DOROTHY MACK
226 The Hungry Heart, ARLENE HALE
227 A Heart Too Proud, LAURA LONDON
228 Love Is the Answer, LOUISE BERGSTROM
229 Love's Untold Secret, BETTY HALE HYATT
230 Tender Longings, BARBARA LYNN
231 Hold Me Forever, MELISSA BLAKELY
232 The Captive Bride, LUCY PHILLIPS STEWART
233 Unexpected Holiday, LIBBY MANSFIELD
234 One Love Forever, MEREDITH BABEAUX BRUCKER
235 Forbidden Yearnings, CANDICE ARKHAM
236 Precious Moments, SUZANNE ROBERTS
237 Surrender to Love, HELEN NUELLE
238 The Heart Has Reasons, STEPHANIE KINCAID
239 The Dancing Doll, JANET LOUISE ROBERTS
240 My Lady Mischief, JANET LOUISE ROBERTS
241 The Heart's Horizons, ANNE SHORE
242 A Lifetime to Love, ANN DABNEY
243 Whispers of the Heart, ANNE SHORE
244 Love's Own Dream, JACQUELINE HACSI
245 La Casa Dorada, JANET LOUISE ROBERTS
246 The Golden Thistle, JANET LOUISE ROBERTS
247 The First Waltz, JANET LOUISE ROBERTS
248 The Cardross Luck, JANET LOUISE ROBERTS
249 The Searching Heart, SUZANNE ROBERTS
250 The Lady Rothschild, SAMANTHA LESTER
251 Bride of Chance, LUCY PHILLIPS STEWART
252 A Tropical Affair, ELISABETH BERESFORD
253 The Impossible Ward, DOROTHY MACK
254 Victim of Love, LEE CANADAY
255 The Bad Baron's Daughter, LAURA LONDON
256 Winter Kisses, Summer Love, ANNE SHORE

WINTER'S LOVING TOUCH

Jacqueline Hacsi

A Candlelight Romance

Published by
Dell Publishing Co., Inc.
1 Dag Hammarskjold Plaza
New York, New York 10017

Copyright © 1979 by Jacqueline Hacsi

All rights reserved. No part of this book may be reproduced or transmitted in any form or by any means, electronic or mechanical, including photocopying, recording or by any information storage and retrieval system, without the written permission of the Publisher, except where permitted by law.

Dell ® TM 681510, Dell Publishing Co., Inc.

ISBN: 0-440-19637-X

Printed in the United States of America

First printing—July 1979

CHAPTER 1

Dr. Carrie Addison, with a companion, stood a little apart from the crowd of grinning, shouting, gesticulating Eskimos who were watching the blanket toss. A woman tourist had volunteered to climb onto the blanket, made of eight walrus-hide skins sewn together, held tautly by a circle of thirty husky Eskimos, and she was now struggling to stay upright while being repeatedly bounced high in the air to the delight of the crowd. The blanket toss was an ancient Eskimo game, said to have originated in order to toss hunters high enough into the air so that they could sight game.

"That looks like so much fun, one of these days I'll get up the nerve to try it myself," Carrie's companion, Leila Parrish, remarked with a grin. Leila was a young woman, tall, buxom, with bright red hair, creamy white skin, a colorful, animated face, and a brash breezy manner. She was a teacher in the local school, and they had met upon Carrie's arrival at Point Hope, Alaska, a few days before.

"If you don't break an arm or a leg trying," Carrie murmured in answer, a slight smile of anxiety curling her mouth. She had enjoyed watching the blanket toss when the villagers, all old hands at it, had taken turns being tossed, but she didn't quite feel as easy watching this now. The woman tourist was young, seemed supple enough, and was not being tossed with too much vigor, but even so Carrie felt it would be far too easy for her to come down too hard or a slight bit awkwardly and sprain an ankle or break a leg. She had heard of this happening with amateurs who threw themselves into the game with too much enthusiasm.

"Well, that's a thought, of course," Leila agreed, but then laughed, as though dismissing the risk, and broke into friendly clapping along with the Eskimos at how well the young woman was doing.

Carrie sighed, momentarily averting her eyes.

It was July Fourth, late afternoon, and for Carrie the daylong festivities were becoming just a slight bit tiring. She had heard but hadn't had prior experience of the fact that no Americans celebrated national Independence Day with more fervent feeling than the native Alaskans. From early morning everyone in the village had joined in one activity after another, either as participant or viewer: kayak racing, Eskimo high jumping, a muktuk eating contest (during which Carrie, along with everyone else, whether contestant or not, had partaken of the chewy delicacy made of whale skin), these games and contests interspersed with frequent exhibitions of Eskimo dancing.

Due to follow after the blanket toss was a parade of the local beauties, which would lead to the choosing of the village queen. After that the feast would begin, to be held in the Parish Hall, with an astonishing variety of foods on hand to be served: ham, caribou stew, whale-meat steaks, bread, doughnuts, a generous assortment of cakes, and the mouth-wateringly delicious Eskimo ice cream, made of caribou fat, seal oil, water, berries and sugar. Last of all, a display of fireworks flown in from the lower states was to be set off against the pale summer sky, with the sun still shining, for at this time of year in Point Hope the sun was visible twenty-four hours a day and would not set again for another few weeks.

As the young woman tourist was tossed up even higher, Carrie, watching again, winced at the sight. Although she had lived in Alaska from the age of five, Carrie was a newcomer to Point Hope, and she still felt very ill at ease. She was twenty-six years old, of average height, and the warm parka and fur-lined trousers she wore concealed a slender, yet curvaceously well-proportioned form. Her oval face, with its fine, delicate features, should have been more attractive than it was; somehow it just missed being beautiful, largely due to a certain paleness, a lack of color or fire. Her light skin was smooth and unblemished, her hair, drawn back tightly from her face and pinned into a bun at the nape of her neck, a rich dark brown. Her large gray eyes were rather anxious and unhappy. About her there was an air of such great shyness and reserve that most people approached her very cautiously, as though to avoid startling or upsetting her. Although she had never in her life been seriously ill, most people who knew her thought of her as rather frail.

As the tossing game drew to a close and the young woman climbed off the blanket, Carrie sighed with relief, momentarily joining in the applause. As she stopped her brief clapping, she felt herself shiver slightly. Aware that she was becoming a bit cold, she lifted her hands to draw her parka hood over her head. As she did so, she saw a young Eskimo boy hurrying up to where she and her companion stood.

"Miss Parrish?" the boy said, panting for breath.

"Yes?" Leila answered, a hint of impatience in her voice as she glanced around.

"The doctor," the boy said hesitantly. "Can doctor come with me, please? At the clinic, two men. They sent me, please. An accident. Bullet wound. Need doctor." The boy punched a finger against his thigh, his eyes darting to Carrie's face. "Doctor come with me, please?" he asked again.

"Of course," Carrie answered, without hesitation. "Excuse me, Leila." She swung around and broke into a quick walk.

The underground in the Arctic stayed frozen the year round, but during the summer months the topsoil defrosted. That didn't mean slush and mud were continually underfoot in Point Hope as was true in much of the Arctic; rather, the ground was covered with a tundra growth of mosses, lichens, and grasses, as well as, in many places, a massed carpet of exquisite wild flowers. This made walking easy and pleasurable, especially in the thick fur-lined boots commonly worn.

As Carrie strode rapidly along, leaving behind the shoreline where the villagers were holding their holiday celebration, heading toward her newly built clinic at the far inland edge of the tiny village, she considered asking the boy if he knew how the accident had happened, whether the two men were hunters from some Eskimo village in the interior or whether the patient was a local villager. But, glancing around, breathing rather heavily from the exertion of walking so fast, Carrie decided against it. As a child and adolescent she had been painfully shy, and only recently, during the last few years, had she begun to overcome this. She still did not find it easy to reach out to others, even to the extent of asking questions. She told herself that they'd soon reach the clinic anyway, then she could get first-hand answers from the men involved, so no use troubling the boy for answers he might not have. Reasoning in this fashion, she hurried along, the boy hurrying along silently at her side.

The village—Point Hope to the outside world, Tigara, meaning index finger to the local inhabitants—was located on a twelve-mile-long sandspit jutting out into the Chukchi Sea. Due to its excellent whaling and hunting, the village had been continuously occupied for more than a thousand years, longer than any other place on the North American continent. The village was now home to more than four hundred Eskimos as well as a handful of Caucasians. In recent years the old sod dwellings had given way to modern frame houses, with living rooms, kitchens, one, two, or three bedrooms, and, while there was no indoor plumbing, there were washrooms equipped with chemical toilets. The houses, which were dotted along the spit of land in no particular pattern, were well insulated, easily kept warm, and wired for electricity. The village was now a fourth-class incorporated city, with a modern school, a fine church, two well-stocked stores, accommodations for a limited number of tourists, and a local coffee shop. To Carrie's eyes, the village seemed like any other very tiny, very modest, suburban town, except displaced to the bleak tundra some 140 miles north of the Arctic Circle.

The majority of the natives depended upon whale,

seal, and caribou hunting for their livelihood as had their forebears for a thousand years. They were a proud, happy, gregarious people who continued to live by their ancient traditions, while at the same time welcoming the gadgets of industrial civilization. The more prosperous village homes boasted electric freezers, stoves, radios, and even tape recorders; dog teams and sleds were giving way more and more to snowmobiles. Tourism was on the increase, becoming an added source of revenue to the village. Of those thousands of people visiting Alaska each year, a certain hearty few eagerly signed up to be flown into Point Hope in order to enjoy the experience of an authentic Eskimo village, a tiny isolated settlement on the very edge of nowhere, as it had seemed to Carrie upon her arrival.

During these first four days she had only a few patients, but this was understandable. It would naturally take a little time for her to earn the trust of the natives, not only those residing in Point Hope but also those clustered in even more isolated groups inland; time for word of a doctor's presence here to spread, to become widely known among the far-flung villages of the Arctic slope. Meanwhile, she planned to circulate among the local people, preaching the wisdom of immunization and inoculation programs for their children, also the availability of medical services for those of any age. This Point Hope clinic was being funded by the federal government, an attempt to make modern medical care available to the most isolated natives.

Reaching the clinic building, Carrie skipped up the three wooden steps, then stopped on the narrow porch. The boy who had been sent to fetch her stood looking up at her momentarily, uncertainly. Then he threw her a little wave and walked off, his mission accomplished.

Startled by his departure, Carrie lifted one hand as though to stop him. It might very well be that the two men awaiting her in the clinic couldn't speak English, in which case the boy could have acted as interpreter. Oh, well, Carrie thought, and squaring her shoulders under her thick warm parka, she put her hand to the doorknob and pushed open the wooden door.

After stepping inside Carrie stopped in surprise, tossing back the hood of her parka. The two men who stood in the small reception room waiting for her weren't natives after all, as she'd taken it for granted they would be. Rather, they were Caucasians. As she hadn't seen either one before, she was certain they didn't live in the village.

"Well—hello," she said. "You sent for me?"

The two men, who had been standing facing each other talking, swung to face her. The larger of the two, a man who stood well over six feet and who looked enormous in his bulky Arctic clothing, caught Carrie's eye first. He stood openly eyeing her, grinning. A man in his early thirties, he had thick curly black hair framing a broad, open, sun and wind-tanned face, with thick straight brows over narrow dark eyes, a fine straight nose, a full, soft-looking mouth. Although he was possibly not quite as conventionally, pretty-boy handsome as her fiance, Mark Slaughter, nevertheless, Carrie thought in surprise, staring across, he had the most attractive face she'd ever seen. In addition, there was about him an air of such overflowing vitality, of barely restrained power and authority, that Carrie felt herself being drawn irresistibly toward him. As she had never felt this way toward any man before, it made her feel instantly nervous and ill at ease.

"Well, hello!" the man echoed her greeting, in a deep, friendly voice. "If we didn't send for you, we most certainly should have. You're a welcome sight indeed after the weeks we've just spent in the back country seeing nothing but mud and slush. I'm Zachary Curtis and this is my young friend and assistant, Matt Sanders."

"How do you do," Carrie managed to murmur in answer, though the man's words had made her feel instantly breathless, as though struck hard in the solar plexus. *Zachary Curtis!* This was a name she had been familiar with for over a year, in the most disagreeable way. Zachary Curtis, the big-shot promoter, president of his own company, En-Ex, Inc., a man who'd piled up a huge fortune roaming the earth exploring for new energy sources, a man who stood for everything that she, as a dedicated environmentalist, bitterly opposed. She'd heard that En-Ex was currently exploring for natural gas reserves here in the north slope area, but still she hadn't expected to meet the company's owner and president. Most certainly she had not expected to come face to face with him in this fashion, within days of her arrival here, before she'd had the least chance to become accustomed to her surroundings. Her inner discomfort grew more pronounced.

"I'm Dr. Carrie Addison," she murmured a moment later, forcing out a small smile. "Which one of you is the patient, please?"

Carrie walked forward. At the far end of the small room was an old wooden table, set up for Carrie's assistant, a middle-aged Eskimo woman named Irvana. In a box on top of this table were the patients' cards Carrie had brought with her. Reaching the table, Carrie pulled a card from the box, sat down on the wooden chair behind the table and picked up a pen.

"Well?" she prodded courteously, lifting her eyes to face the two men when neither one answered.

Again her eyes went first to the larger man, and irritation spurted through her as she caught his dark, piercing eyes staring down at her. His broad, boyish grin had all but completely faded away, and his eyes, it seemed to Carrie, gleamed now with a faint hint of hostility, which caused an answering wave of hostility to run through her.

In annoyance she forced her eyes to move to the second, smaller man, the one Zachary Curtis had introduced as Matt Sanders. Matt was a man of about average height, probably quite slender under his bulky clothing, a man in his middle twenties with a thin, sensitive looking face, light hazel eyes, a sprinkling of freckles. As her eyes moved to him, Matt smiled rather nervously at her, but still didn't speak to answer her simple question.

In even greater annoyance, Carrie moved her eyes back to Zachary Curtis. "Look," she said, "the boy who brought me here said that one of you has a bullet wound in his thigh. I'd like to fill out a card for whichever one of you that is. So which one is it?"

As her question died away, Carrie saw the two men exchange a quick glance, Matt hurriedly looking around at Curtis as though requesting permission to speak. Permission was apparently denied for Matt's thin face flushed slightly and his eyes dropped. Zachary Curtis, once again smiling broadly, stepped forward, and seated himself on a wooden chair in front of the small table. Leaning forward, he pinned Carrie down under his piercing gaze.

"Well, before we get to that," he said, in his soft, deep voice, "could you please tell us where the doctor is and how soon we might expect him here? It's quite possible we haven't the time to wait and will have to go elsewhere."

"Go elsewhere?" Carrie echoed, feeling herself grow even more angry. Not a minute before she had introduced herself as the doctor and felt sure that Zachary Curtis had heard her do so. "Where else did you think you might go? There's no other doctor anywhere in the area."

Grinning across at her, his dark green eyes narrowing almost into slits, Zachary shrugged.

"Depends on how you define area," he responded. "Our plane's out on the airstrip and we can always get back in it and hop over to the hospital in Kotzebue, or even go on down to Nome. On the other hand—" he shrugged again, "—we would really rather wait for the doctor here, especially if you'd be kind enough to let us know how soon we might expect him."

Flushing with anger, Carrie announced coldly, "*I* am the doctor, Mr. Curtis, and have already introduced myself as such. If one of you wants and needs medical attention, fine, let's get on with it. If not, I'd like to close the clinic up again and return to enjoy the holiday celebration. So which one of you is it?"

As her voice died away, she gazed coldly across at the man sitting on the other side of the table from her, then she circled her eyes around to the young Matt Sanders. Again neither man answered. Ready to burst with angry frustration, Carrie slid the patient card back into the box, deciding that she had wasted all the time she was going to on these two infuriating men.

She stood up, and as she did so Zachary Curtis stood up too. As Carrie glanced his way, it seemed to her that she caught a little grimace of pain as he pushed himself to his feet, also a slight favoring of his right leg as though that was the source of his pain. So he's the one! she thought, a quick spurt of excitement racing through her. This handsome, powerful, arrogant man had a bullet lodged in his leg, a wound that was clearly bothering him, yet apparently he was too much of a male chauvinist to allow a woman doctor to treat him. What did medical ethics suggest that she do?

Instead of stepping around the table and departing, Carrie hesitated and considered reseating herself, which would give Curtis the chance to sit down again too. But before she had done this, Zachary placed his hands down on the tabletop and leaned forward over it, his handsome face grinning boyishly at her.

"Could you possibly answer my question, young lady?" he said. "My friend and I really would like to see the doctor. Are you perchance the nurse here? Or the doctor's wife? In either case, can you give us some idea when the doctor will arrive?"

"I told you—*I'm* the doctor!" Carrie cried, losing control of her temper. Her ordinarily pale gray eyes flashed fire as she stared across at this outrageous, bullying man; she could feel the red race up her ordinarily pale, cool cheeks. Breathing hard, her chest rising and falling rapidly with anger, Carrie stared directly across into the piercing green eyes which were staring so relentlessly at her. Then suddenly she saw those same eyes begin to twinkle outrageously as

Zachary Curtis drew a little away and burst out laughing. He had deliberately provoked her in this fashion solely to enrage her!

Carrie drew herself up stiffly, doing her best to recompose herself. She had lost her temper so few times in her life, she felt outraged that it had happened now. Dropping her eyes, she stared unseeingly down, then a moment later sank down again on the chair behind the table, again picking out a card from the box.

As soon as she had reseated herself, Zachary Curtis sat down again too, again with a slight grimace of pain. His laugh dying away, he faced her with a grin, but a grin that didn't reach his gleaming dark eyes which settled on her with a coolly appraising look.

"Forgive me, Dr. Addison," he said, in a voice as arrogant as ever, with no hint of real apology in it. "Sometimes I let my perverse sense of humor run away with me, I'm afraid. Matt and I heard a few days ago that the new doctor here in Point Hope was a woman, and this so struck our fancy that when we had a few hours off today we decided to fly over to meet you. Again, I'm sorry."

"No need to apologize," Carrie murmured stiffly, her eyes down as she wrote in the name *Zachary Curtis* on the card. Nervously lifting her eyes again, she asked, as pleasantly as she could manage, "All right, Mr. Curtis, how old are you, please?" Rather than ask again which man had the wound, she was going to proceed as though Zachary had already admitted that he was the one, as indeed his grimace of pain, which she'd now caught twice, *had* admitted. If he'd just answer a few simple questions . . .

But again Zachary didn't answer. Instead he pushed to his feet and when Carrie's eyes rose in surprise, she saw that he was smiling again, not his wide boyish grin, but a small friendly smile that reached all the way into his eyes, filling them with warmth and caring.

"Tear up the card, doctor, please. Matt and I came to meet you, to satisfy our curiosity about the new woman doctor in this godforsaken place, that's all. Neither of us needs any medical care. As you can see, we are both perfectly healthy men."

Pulse pounding hard, Carrie stood up too, trying to make sure she did not again lose her temper. "What I've seen, Mr. Curtis," she answered, "is that you wince with pain when you change position or put any sudden weight on your right leg. The boy who came for me told me that one of you has a bullet wound in his thigh and I don't question that this is the case. If you don't want me to fill out a card, all right, we'll skip it. Just step inside to my treatment room and we'll have a look."

Carrie swung from the table and stepped toward the door leading from the waiting room, her hand out to open the door. As she did so, she could see the two men exchange a quick glance, though neither made the least move to follow her. It occurred to her that the best thing to do was to leave them alone for a minute; let argue out the problem, whatever it was, in private. Therefore she murmured, "Excuse me a moment, please," opened the door leading into the adjoining treatment room, and stepped through it, closing it immediately behind her. If they responded by walking out, so be it. If Zachary Curtis was determined not to accept treatment from a woman doctor, there was no way she could force him to do so.

Sighing, Carrie walked aimlessly forward in the treatment room. Reaching the back wall where the cupboards were, she swung around and walked idly forward again. As she approached the door leading out to the waiting room, she became aware that she could hear the two men's voices. Without conscious decision to do so, she stopped walking and listened, tensing at the words she heard.

"Zack, can't you see what a blasted fool you're being!" Matt Sanders was saying. "You know what a time you've been having with that leg, the devil's own time—why else did we break off and fly here today? And to come all the way here and then turn down treatment just because the doctor happens to be a woman—Zack, that's crazy! Now go on in there."

Zachary's voice cut in, full and deep. "But it isn't because she's a woman, Matt, that's got nothing to do with it. I've got nothing against a woman's being a doctor. But that particular woman . . ."

A momentary silence, and then Zachary went on in an even lower voice as Carrie listened in shock. "Not because she's a woman, Matt, but because of the woman she is. Surely you noticed her eyes, the coldest eyes I've ever seen. Don't you understand, Matt? I'm *afraid* to let her touch me, afraid I'll wind up with frostbite if I do. You know me, Matt, know that I can stand a good deal of cold, but that woman, that degree of coldness—I just don't know. I'd almost rather endure the pain I've already got than risk being treated by a woman as hate-filled and hostile as that!"

Momentarily Carrie felt too frozen to move, then she forced herself to swing around and walk again toward the back of the room, her ears ringing with shock over what she had heard. *Not because she's a woman, Matt, but because of the woman she is. Cold. Hate filled. Hostile.*

Again reaching the back of the room, facing the

cupboards, Carrie came to a stop, tense with shock. She was suddenly startled to hear the door to the treatment room opening. Swinging around, she saw Zachary stride in. He threw her a friendly little smile.

"All right, doctor, here I am. I do have a wound in my leg, the result of a hunting accident, and would like your help. Shall I undress?"

Trembling in spite of her best effort not to, Carrie reached for a clean white gown neatly folded in a cupboard and tossed it across. "Yes, please do. Then put this on and get on the table. I'll be right with you." Carrie swung around to face the cupboards again, busying herself getting down supplies she might need.

A few minutes later, when she swung back around, she saw that Zachary had already disrobed and lay on the table on his abdomen, wearing the gown. She walked over, pushed the gown up a bit, and saw that the wound was in the back of the right thigh just an inch or so above the back of the knee, with a clean appearance and the bullet embedded not at all deeply in the flesh. As she set to work, she tried to drive out of her thoughts who this man was, everything that had happened, every word she'd heard said. For now he was simply a nameless, faceless patient who needed her help.

Before long she had the bullet extracted. She bandaged the wound and administered two preventive shots. As she worked over him, Zachary kept his head down and he did not say a word. When she indicated to him that she was finished and that he could get up and dress, he lifted his head and glanced around with a smile.

"Doctor," he said, his dark eyes meeting hers, "you

have the most amazingly gentle touch, the softest hands I've ever felt."

"Oh?" Carrie responded, then burst out with a surprised, pleased little laugh. "Then I didn't give you frostbite after all, as you feared I would?" Her back was to him as she said this, as she walked to the cupboards to put her supplies away.

"You overheard us then? I'm sorry you did."

"No matter." Carrie busied herself putting everything away. By the time she had finished and turned back around, she found that Zachary had dressed and stood leaning against the treatment table. As their eyes met, Carrie felt a little leap of excitement run through her.

Handing him a tube of salve and some bandaging material, she gave him brief instructions on how to take care of his wound.

"Well, that's it, Mr. Curtis, you're free to leave now. And I really would like to get back to the holiday celebration."

"So how much do I owe you?" Zachary asked, his hand going into his trousers pocket.

"Oh, there's no charge," Carrie said quickly. "This is a federally funded clinic, free of charge to everyone. I'm only glad I could be of help."

Zachary straightened up from leaning against the table, but still made no move to leave. "Then there's no way I can show my gratitude?" he asked, his dark eyes holding hers.

"Of course there is," Carrie responded instantly with a smile. "By having your wound heal properly." She walked on by him, opened the door of the treatment room and stepped out quickly, hoping that her patient would pick up the hint and follow her. Now that she had given all the medical treatment indicated, she wished to be free of this man. He was still Zachary Curtis, a man whose name she had learned to despise long before ever meeting him.

CHAPTER 2

Four days later Carrie saw Zachary Curtis again.

Leila Parrish had invited her to dinner that evening. Leila lived in a new, one-bedroom, frame house, comfortably furnished, only a few hundred yards from the village school.

For dinner Leila fixed them soup with rice, macaroni, and reindeer meat, and had baked some fresh yeast doughnuts. As they sat in the kitchen eating, Leila remarked, "This is standard village fare, Carrie, which you might as well get used to. Of course, it isn't always reindeer meat. There's also fish, whale, or caribou."

"But rarely any vegetables," Carrie murmured. "That much I've learned so far."

After dinner they decided to go for a stroll. As they walked, Leila mentioned that the most exciting time of the year in Point Hope was in the spring, when the ice in the Chukchi Sea began breaking up, forming leads—channels through the ice—and the northern migration of the big bowhead whales began.

"Does the village stir with excitement then!" Leila exclaimed. "The women spend their days recovering the wooden boat frames with sealskin. The paddles are cleaned, smoothed, and made ready, the sealskin floats inflated, the harpoons carefully oiled and cleaned.

"The whole village thinks of nothing else," Leila continued. "The big bowheads are coming through—to be hunted by a dozen fearless natives from a little wooden paddle boat the same way that Eskimos here have hunted and brought back whales for over a thousand years. When a whale is sighted coming through—well, that's an exciting time for everyone here, I'll tell you!"

They had turned back and were almost to the school building, where Leila was about to bid her goodnight, when Carrie heard a man's stride approaching. Glancing up she saw that the man was Zachary Curtis, bearing down upon them with a broad, friendly smile.

Carrie stopped walking, so Leila did too.

Within a few seconds Zachary had reached them and stopped before them, smiling even more broadly.

"Good evening, Dr. Carrie. A lovely evening, isn't it?"

"Yes, yes, it is." Carrie noticed again what a vibrantly attractive face Zachary had. She also felt assaulted once more by his vitality, as though it was a living thing that could reach across the space separating them and draw her irresistibly toward him, and this again made her feel nervously uneasy.

"Leila, this is Zachary Curtis, a—a patient of mine. Mr. Curtis, Leila Parrish, one of the teachers in the school here."

"Mr. Curtis, what a pleasure!" Leila exclaimed. "I've heard about you, knew you were up here in the north slope area exploring for gas, but I didn't expect to meet you. Is this your first visit here?"

"No, my second," Zachary answered easily in his soft, full voice. "I was here a few days ago, on the Fourth, at which time Dr. Carrie was kind enough to treat me for a minor medical problem I had. For which I thank you once again," he added, his dark eyes swinging around to search out Carrie's.

"Did you fly in just now?" Leila asked. "We noticed a plane coming in. Was that you?"

"It was," Zachary acknowledged.

With a little laugh Leila moved flirtatiously toward him. Her parka hood was thrown back, her bright red hair shining brightly in the early evening light. As she stepped toward Zachary, smiling, she looked extraordinarily pretty, it seemed to Carrie.

"Then, Mr. Curtis," Leila said, tilting her head, "do I dare ask you for a very great favor? Do you ever take people up in your plane for a scenic view of the area? I've been here two years now and have only been up once, very briefly, apart from my flights in and out, of course, and surely there is no sight in the world more fantastic than the Brooks Range from the air. I know this is being terribly forward but this has meant so much to me for so long." Tilting her head, Leila smiled up at Zachary, batting her thick, mascaraed lashes. "I'd appreciate it so much, Mr. Curtis, I can't tell you how much!"

Grinning again, Zachary responded at once, gallantly, "Of course, Miss Parrish, I'd be most happy to take you. And possibly—" his eyes circled around to search out Carrie's again, "—Dr. Carrie would be interested in going too?"

"Thank you," Carrie murmured nervously, meeting his eyes for only a second before she hurriedly circled her gaze away, "but I don't think so. Thank you anyway."

"But, Carrie, why not?" Leila said. "It's a fantastic sight, believe me. Or are you afraid of flying, is that it?" Without waiting for an answer, she rushed on to say to Zachary, "If you really mean it, Mr. Curtis, and I certainly hope you do, I'm going to hold you to it, believe me. To have your own private plane in this area—I've often thought that's what everyone up here needs, the same way you need a car in the lower states. But, unfortunately, most of us have to do without."

Feeling increasingly uncomfortable, Carrie broke in to murmur, "Well, I—I feel I should be getting home. Thank you for the dinner, Leila, and I—I'll see you again." With this she turned and began walking quickly off.

Sha hadn't gone twenty yards when she heard a heavy stride following. Glancing around she saw that Zachary was walking rapidly after her. Within seconds he had caught up and was following along at her side.

"Well—Mr. Curtis," Carrie said, in as self-possessed a voice as she could manage. "I was under the impression that you were busily exploring quite some distance away from here, and I really did not expect to see you again."

"You didn't?" There was mockery in his voice. As Carrie glanced quickly around, she saw that his gleaming dark eyes were steadily fixed on her.

Dropping her eyes, Carrie walked hurriedly along in silence, wishing that the man beside her would say goodnight and depart. What did he want of her anyway?

Without explaining his reason for doing so, Zachary

continued to walk along at her side, not speaking, until at length Carrie could not tolerate the uneasiness this caused in her a moment longer.

"So—did you come back to Point Hope for some particular reason?" she asked. While she rarely felt at ease with people unless she knew them extremely well, her discomfort in the company of this man seemed to her the strongest she'd ever experienced. If he had some reason for bothering her like this, how she wished he'd come out with it and then leave her in peace!

"Yes, I did have a particular reason," Zachary said, turning to face her, unsmiling. They both stopped walking and stood facing each other, Zachary's dark eyes intently fixed on her face. After a pronounced pause he added in his soft full voice, "A very particular reason—to see you again."

"Oh," Carrie said, her pulse giving another hard little leap, though she did her best not to betray the wildly chaotic feelings his explanation caused in her. Somehow she'd known he would say this. But why had he wanted to see her again?

For a moment she stood looking straight up into his gleaming dark eyes, then with a little shiver she hurriedly dropped her eyes again. Squaring her shoulders resolutely under her parka, she began walking forward again, certain that Zachary would once again fall into step beside her, which he did.

"So—for what possible reason did you wish to see me again?" she asked finally, striding along even more quickly, as though in this way she might possibly outdistance her nervousness, the great inner discomfort Zachary's presence caused in her. When he didn't answer for quite some time, Carrie, tensing even worse, glanced around, noticing at once his broad, boyish grin, the teasing glint in his dark green eyes.

Again they stopped walking. Zachary stood there before her, some three feet away, the hood of his light tan parka thrown back, his thick curly black hair gleaming in the pale evening sunlight. His broad handsome face, tanned to a bright, burnished look, was almost expressionless except for a very slight smile playing around the corners of his full, soft-looking mouth. His dark green eyes, under the thick black brows, were more open than usual, and they gazed steadily down at Carrie with an amused warmth that made her feel instantly even more uncomfortable.

"You know for what reason," Zachary murmured after a moment, as though he found it amusing that she had asked.

As she stood looking up at him, nervously blinking, something in Carrie's fingers ached to reach up and stroke the polished skin of his cheeks, then test the softness of his soft-looking mouth. She immediately tensed against this ache, drawing herself up even more stiffly.

"You're mistaken, Mr. Curtis," she said, in as cool and calm a voice as she could manage. "I'm afraid I haven't the least idea why you're here."

"Because you're a doctor," Zachary said, his smile rippling with even more amusement across his mouth. "And the nearest doctor around, the only one in this area, as you mentioned, that's why I've come to see you again."

"Oh," Carrie said, dropping her eyes, feeling instantly, sharply deflated. She began walking forward again, more slowly, Zachary once again falling into step beside her. "Your leg is giving you trouble, is that what you mean?"

"No, no, not in the slightest," Zachary said. "I didn't mean that. But I've changed the bandage each day, as you instructed, and the fact is I've already run out of bandages. Two of the other men had slight accidents, nothing serious, but between us we've used up everything you gave me so I came back hoping you'd be able to sell me a bit more."

"Oh," Carrie murmured, feeling even more deflated. She walked along in silence after that, Zachary beside her. Soon they reached the small, frame building which housed her clinic and ascended the steps onto the narrow porch. As she opened the door and stepped inside, she motioned for her companion to follow.

Carrie quickly crossed the room and went into the treatment room, Zachary following. There she drew off her parka and, without glancing his way, picked up a clean dressing gown, tossed it to him, and remarked casually, "Take off your clothes, please, and I'll have a look at your leg." She walked to the rear of the room and opened a cupboard to begin getting down some material.

Zachary burst out with a brief laugh. "Really, doctor," he said, "the leg is doing just fine. I really don't see that it needs to have you look at it. If you'll just let me have another tube of that salve, plus a few bandages—" His voice died away as he stood looking across at her, a slight embarrassment gleaming in his eyes.

Instantly annoyed, Carrie snapped irritably, "Mr. Curtis, it's obvious that you persist in thinking of me first of all as a woman—"

"And an extremely pretty woman at that," Zachary threw in, with a sudden broad grin.

"—but I am nevertheless a fully accredited doctor as well, and your resistance to treatment, not just today, but the other day in particular, is not only incredibly chauvinistic, it is in addition an insult to the training I've had and to all the years of hard work and study I've put in. If you think I have the least personal interest in you—"

"Haven't you?" he interrupted.

"—you are very much mistaken. To me you are simply a patient who needs attention, and before I give you any more supplies, I must insist you allow me to check your wound."

Before these words had quite died away, Zachary stepped forward, swept her up against him, and without warning pressed his full, grinning mouth down on hers. Momentarily too startled even to fight, Carrie felt the warmth of his lips crushing hers, and as her pulse leaped wildly, she felt an urge to press herself in against him even more closely, to melt against the powerful warmth of his body, to become a part of his incredible strength and vitality. Instantly frightened by these thoughts, Carrie stiffened and began struggling angrily to free herself, lifting her arms in an attempt to break Zachary's hold on her. Within a few moments, with a little laugh, Zachary let go and stepped back, grinning across at her.

"How dare you?" Carrie cried, in fury lifting her hand to press the back of it against her mouth to wipe off any remnants of his assault. "If you think that proves anything, apart from the fact you're bigger than I am—"

"I wasn't trying to *prove* anything, doctor." Again there was mockery in his voice as his dark eyes danced. "I was merely trying to shut you up. Whether you know it or not, whether you dare face it yet or not, you *do* have a personal interest in me, a very strong personal interest in me, just as I have in you.

For the moment, however, if you insist upon having another look at my leg, so be it. Whatever the doctor orders, doctor."

With a mocking little smile, Zachary walked toward the treatment table, already beginning to undress, while Carrie, trembling, turned toward the cupboards to draw out supplies.

After she heard Zachary climb onto the table, she took in a deep breath, swung around, and walked over to him. Again he lay face down on the table, wearing the white dressing gown. As she bent over him, Carrie blushed with the memory of what he had said on his earlier visit, that she had the gentlest hands he'd ever had touch him, and remembering this made her feel selfconscious and nervous right when she most needed, and wanted, to feel cool and competent. Oh, what an unsettling, infuriating man this was!

Carefully pulling away the bandaging material, Carrie saw instantly, with relief, that Zachary was right, the wound was healing very nicely, with no sign of infection. In short order she had a fresh bandage securely in place. After pulling down the dressing gown, without thinking she gave his leg a friendly little pat, saying, "All right, Mr. Curtis, everything's fine. You can dress now."

Zachary's head lifted at once and his eyes swung around. One hand shot out to catch her hand. Carrie tensed with certainty that he meant to swing up now and grab her again—and how she would fight him if he did!—but all he did was say quietly, with a soft warm smile, "Thank you, doctor. You're not only very gentle, you're really very sweet."

Trembling again, Carrie drew her hand free, swinging quickly away. "Nonsense," she said brusquely. "I'm only doing my job." She walked hurriedly back to the cupboard again and stood there, her back to the room, while Zachary climbed off the table and dressed.

She had unwrapped a lengthy strip of heavy bandaging, snipped it off the main roll, then rerolled it neatly. She took down some gauze and cut off a generous supply of that, storing the material in a small cardboard box. After adding a tube of antiseptic salve, she turned around, walked to Zachary and extended the box toward him.

"Here you are. I'm pleased the leg is doing so well, but if it should give you any trouble in the future, which I truly don't think it will, feel free to drop by again and I'll gladly do whatever I can."

"Thank you, Carrie." Zachary stood leaning back against the table, his eyes steadily meeting hers. A moment later he said, "There's something I'm tremendously curious about, Dr. Carrie. How did a woman like you, doctor or no, ever happen to wind up in a godforsaken place like this, miles away from anything? I've wondered about that ever since I first saw you four days ago."

Carrie's eyes flashed up to challenge his. "Really, Mr. Curtis, I don't see that that's any business of yours. Now that you have your supplies, I suggest you leave. Please just go!" she added, even more irritably, glaring up at him.

Zachary pushed forward, drawing up to his full height. As a look crossed his face that told her he might have it in mind to grab her again, to force another kiss upon her, Carrie quickly stepped back, breathing hard, trying to put a warning into her eyes that he'd better not try. He wouldn't again take her by surprise. From now on she'd be on her guard and would fight against any embrace he tried to force on her.

31

With a little sigh Zachary dropped his gaze and half turned away. "All right, I'm leaving, and thanks for these things." He glanced back. "But I haven't yet paid you for them."

"Never mind, it's quite all right," Carrie said quickly. "Just take them and go, please." With that she turned her back on him and again walked toward the wall cabinets.

She heard his steps as he left, heard the outside door open and close and knew he was gone. Thank goodness! she thought. She set about putting away the bandage rolls and other things she'd gotten out. Hopefully it was all over now and she'd never have to face that unsettling man again!

After she'd gotten everything neatly put away, Carrie turned from the cupboard, wishing she had more to do to occupy herself. It was only about eight in the evening and she really wasn't very tired yet or ready for bed.

She left the treatment room, going through the door that led to her living quarters, which occupied the right half of the same frame building.

Just as her clinic had two small rooms, so did her living quarters. The forward room, the equivalent of the tiny waiting room on the left side of the building, she had furnished as a living room. Behind this room was a larger room, the equivalent of the treatment room on the other side of the building, and this larger room she had furnished as her bedroom-kitchen. Against the back wall she had a narrow cot upon which she slept. An old fiberboard cupboard was against the interior wall; inside the cupboard was a small chest of drawers in which she kept her underthings. A small stove was against the outer wall, placed under the only window; alongside it was a sink of sorts, one that did not have running water, of course, but which she nevertheless could use to prepare her food and wash her cooking utensils with water brought in by bucket from outside. Up here in the Arctic, water was the least of anyone's problems. The biggest problem for her, at least so far, was the strong feeling of being displaced, not feeling at home, of loneliness.

She had spent most of her evenings alone so far, here in her bedroom-kitchen. Though she'd met the few Caucasians who lived in the village, and they'd all been extremely courteous, inviting her to visit them, she had never been one to make friends easily, had always felt ill at ease among strangers, and consequently found it preferable to spend most of her time alone. But it did get lonely.

Sighing, Carrie entered her bedroom-kitchen after Zachary left, wishing she had something useful or entertaining to do. She walked to her bed, plunked down on it, then leaned down to unstrap and kick off her boots. She absently picked up the newspaper clipping she had dug out a few days before, just after Zachary's first visit, a clipping she had dropped onto the hooked rug alongside the bed just that morning after rereading it for about the twelfth time.

It was quite a lengthy article, published in a paper in Anchorage, an article her fiance had given her to read just before he'd left for Washington, D.C., early that spring. For four years Mark had worked with a commission set up to determine which areas in the state of Alaska should be set aside and protected as wilderness areas, and he was now in the national capital lobbying for passage of the bill that had been written and introduced into Congress as a result of the commission's work, a bill known as the Udall Wilderness Areas bill. As a consequence of his work, she and Mark were now geographically about as far apart as they could get and still be in the same country, but they kept as closely in touch with each other as they could, writing almost daily. Frowning, Carrie began to scan the newspaper article, looking again—though she knew it by heart by now—for the reference to Zachary Curtis.

Finding it, she narrowed her eyes on the small print and read the sentence for about the twentieth time. Though Zachary was mentioned by name, and identified as president of his own rapidly expanding company, En-Ex, Inc., a company specializing in the worldwide exploration for energy sources, very little was written about him, just that he belonged to a committee of millionaire businessmen who had banded together to fight the Udall Wilderness Areas bill. Everything that her fiance was fighting to bring about —the very things that aware, concerned, intelligent people like Mark were struggling to achieve—greedy, selfish, self-centered men like Zachary Curtis were equally determined to thwart and destroy. Oversized, ruthless bully! Carrie thought, and in disgust she tossed the newspaper back down.

Feeling bored and lonely, she flopped down full length on her bed. Before long she drifted off into a light sleep. She'd slept only a few minutes, however, before a loud pounding on her door abruptly awakened her. Jerking upright, feeling a slight bit dazed, she called out, "Yes, yes, who is it?" This was the first time anyone had knocked on the door to her personal quarters, much less pounded as though to knock the door down. "I'll be right there."

After hastily sticking her stockinged feet back into her boots, she stood up, frantically wondering what kind of medical emergency had arisen, for surely it had to be that—why else would anyone have pounded so imperiously on her door? She hurried over to the door and pulled it open, and in surprise found herself staring at an empty room. Where in the world had the person gotten to, or had she only imagined that frenzied pounding on her door?

"Hi, I'm out here," a man's voice called then, a voice she instantly recognized and which made her nearly burst with anger. How dared he return so soon after she'd requested that he leave? Not only return, but come into her treatment room and pound noisily on the door of her private quarters? Who did he think he was anyway?

Striding quickly across the room, Carrie shook with righteous anger. She stepped through the doorway into the tiny waiting room ready to let loose with a few choice epithets. If this infuriating man would not of his own accord stop bedeviling her . . .

Eyes flashing, cheeks on fire, she stopped walking, glaring across at Zachary as he sat once again on the chair in front of Irvana's table.

"All right, Mr. Curtis, I've about had it with you!" she cried in fury. "How dare you come charging in here to pound on my door like that? If I thought for one minute you had a legitimate excuse—but I know you haven't, that you're simply being your usual, thoughtless, arrogant self! And now if you would kindly just leave again—"

Gesturing furiously toward the door, Carrie stopped yelling, having run of breath. Panting, she stood alongside the table, still furiously glaring out her anger and disgust.

Zachary rose slowly to his feet, grinning. "God but you're pretty when you're angry. Eyes flashing fire like that, you're beautiful." He stepped forward toward her, warm eyes threatening to envelop her again, arms out as though of a mind to grab her and once again crush her against him.

"Don't you dare!" Carrie squealed, her voice catching nervously. She stepped hurriedly behind the small wooden table, breathing even harder. "I very strongly dislike you, Mr. Curtis, don't you understand that?" she cried. "There's nothing about you I can even tolerate, let alone like. The crazy idea you seem to have that I am personally interested in you is so far off base as to be absolutely ludicrous. I consider you selfish, self-centered, arrogant, ruthless, a ruthless exploiter of the earth for your own selfish ends. The fact is I thoroughly despise you, Mr. Curtis!"

Carrie stopped only long enough to catch her breath, and then, drawing herself up to her full height, she snapped out, "Hopefully I have now made myself sufficiently clear, and I wish you to leave!"

"Right," Zachary said, flashing her a small, amused smile. "Believe me, I will. But the reason I came back—well, it occurred to me I'd forgotten to mention something I meant to tell you, something I believe you'll be happy to hear."

He paused a moment, smiling even more broadly, and then went on, with an apologetic little shrug, "Or maybe I didn't exactly forget to tell you, maybe I just wanted an excuse to return after you told me to leave.

"Anyway," he added, "yesterday I moved my base of operations from up around Barrow to only a few miles up the coast from here, and I did this for one reason only, because you're here, a qualified medical doctor, so that my men and I and our families will be able to get medical attention more quickly in the future if we need it. This is only a five minute hop by plane now from where we are."

"You—you did?" Carrie was so startled she stuttered. "You—you moved your camp simply to be closer to me?"

"To bring my people closer to medical care should we need it," Zachary said. "Yes, doctor, I did. Not that this is going to mean a lot of business for you right off. The crew I've got with me is made up of healthy young men who aren't apt to need a doctor too often, but at the same time," he added with a little shrug, "accidents do happen, in fact they happen quite frequently, and it will be comforting to know we're only a few minutes away from competent medical care."

"Well—well, thank you," Carrie murmured in confusion, her face feeling even more flushed. With great effort she managed to raise her eyes up, to meet his. "I—I appreciate this show of trust in me, truly I do."

"Think nothing of it," Zachary said, with a small friendly smile. "The first glimpse I had of you four days ago I knew instantly that here was an intelligent, trustworthy doctor." After a slight pause he added, in a faintly teasing tone, "Cold and not very friendly, but competent. But then I told myself," he added, his smile dying away as his piercing dark eyes stared at her, "that the right man could warm you up."

Eyes flashing up, Carrie tensed painfully again. "Please, Mr. Curtis," she said irritably, "let's not get into that again. I appreciate what you've done—about moving your camp, I mean—but what I said a minute ago still goes. I don't have the least personal interest in you, never have had, never will have. It seems obvious to me that we are not now and never will be in the slightest degree compatible, and while I will be most happy to provide medical treatment for any of your men who might need it—"

"How about the women?" Zachary interrupted, an irrepressible grin once again spreading across his face. "Two of my regular employees have their wives with them, and several of the Eskimos have not only their wives but their children. Altogether we have over fifty people in our camp."

"Is your wife there too?" Carrie asked, not intending to say any such thing. Instantly appalled at herself, she bit furiously at her lower lip as though in punishment for having allowed that question to slip past.

"My wife?" Zachary laughed. His eyes warmly on her, he murmured, "My dear sweet Carrie, I don't have a wife." The next moment he leaned forward and managed to brush his lips against her cheek.

Cheeks afire, Carrie jerked away, fury pouring through her.

"Damnit, Mr. Curtis, I told you to cut that out! What does it take to discourage you anyway, for God's sake? Didn't you just hear what I told you, that I thoroughly detest everything about you and want nothing whatsoever to do with you? If you insist upon forcing yourself upon me like this, I'll have to take some kind of action to stop you. But a man with the least sensitivity would have ceased offering such unwanted attentions long before now!"

"What about you?" Zachary asked, drawing back. "Are you married, Carrie?"

Her angry eyes flashing across at him, Carrie answered quickly, "Not at the moment, but I *am* engaged and soon will be married. Right now my fiance happens to be in Washington, D.C., where he's working toward passage of the Wilderness Areas bill." She threw this in proudly. "But just because we happen to be temporarily separated geographically does not mean we are not completely devoted to one another. And if you don't leave me alone in the future, I may find that I have to complain to him, and I might mention that his family moved to Alaska almost three decades ago and Mark has many, many influential friends who would be very greatly annoyed to hear that I have had to put up with this kind of molestation. Surely a word to the wise is sufficient, I trust?" Carrie ended on a cool, confident note, her eyes still daring to challenge his.

Looking steadily across at her, unsmiling, Zachary said, in a thoughtful voice, "So your boyfriend's an environmentalist, is he? I suppose that means that you are too."

Carrie nodded instantly, emphatically, hopefully to get it through to this man once and for all where her sympathies lay.

A small scornful smile pulled on Zachary's mouth. A moment later he added, in the same thoughtful voice, "Well, now I'm beginning to see the full dimensions of the problem, at least, which is always a necessary first step. Good day, my sweet, beautiful Carrie, I'll see you soon again," and with that he swung away and strode rapidly across the tiny room. He exited through the door, carefully closing it behind him, the sound of the door's closing soon dying away in the still, small room.

My God, what does it take to discourage that man? Carrie thought in dismay, staring across at the closed door. But at this point he's surely only bluffing, she assured herself, and with that thought she sank down on the chair behind the table, feeling suddenly so exhausted she wasn't sure she could stay upright a moment longer.

Surely, in spite of his final words, Zachary Curtis would never come by to bother her again.

CHAPTER 3

Two evenings later Carrie saw Zachary again.

She'd had a busy, satisfying day. A dozen village women had brought their children in for general check-ups and preventive shots, and three of the women had lingered to discuss medical problems of their own. In the late afternoon as her last patient left, Carrie felt elated, happier than she'd felt since her arrival in Point Hope.

After making her final notation on a patient chart, Carrie wandered into her living quarters. She was hungry, but she decided suddenly that she didn't feel like cooking. Why not go to the village coffee shop for dinner? It was another lovely summer day, clear, crisp, clean, and it would do her good to get outside to stretch her legs.

After washing herself and pulling on a soft warm parka, Carrie headed outside. As she was walking toward the main part of the village, she decided, on impulse, to go by Leila's and invite her along as her guest. She owed Leila a dinner, and this would give her a chance to discharge her social obligation.

As she neared the school, she turned to walk to Leila's house, but upon arriving there and knocking, she found no one home. Maybe Leila was already at the coffee shop and she'd be able to join her there.

When she arrived at the coffee shop, however, she saw no sign of Leila, nor was there anyone there she knew even slightly. Feeling somewhat selfconscious, she ordered a dinner of soup, fish, and coffee, with yeast doughnuts and frozen Eskimo ice cream for dessert. After she'd finished this, eating slowly and carefully, her eyes down, she ordered a second cup of steaming hot coffee, which she sipped down very slowly, reluctant to have to leave.

All too soon, though, the last drop of her coffee was gone, and Carrie, with a sigh, paid for her dinner and left, walking slowly back toward the clinic. She had just passed the school building when she heard people off to her left, heard a loud burst of rich happy laughter, and glancing down toward Leila's house she saw the source of the laughter: Leila, Zachary, and Matt Sanders were walking away from Leila's house, heading toward where she was.

Carrie's first impulse, as her cheeks flushed and her eyes darted quickly away, was to hurry forward as rapidly as possible and in this way avoid meeting or being seen by the trio. But she'd gone only a step or two when Leila called out in a loud, cheerful voice, "Hey, Carrie, wait up. Wait right there!" and Carrie, her step faltering, then stopping, felt she had no choice but to do as Leila had ordered.

She swung to face the three people approaching her, and noticed at once, with a slight dip of her pulse, that Leila was striding along so close to Zachary that her body kept pressing his; her arm was possessively wound through his. Matt was on Leila's other side, but five or six feet away, and his narrow, lightly freckled face looked a slight bit embarrassed.

"Oh, Carrie, you should have come along!" Leila cried in greeting as the three arrived where Carrie was and stopped. "You really should have. Zack took me up in his plane this afternoon, and you never saw such fantastic scenery! We were up for hours, out over the Brooks Range, then back along the coast. Utterly fantastic! Why didn't you come along?"

Well, for one thing, Carrie thought in dismay as she tried to smile politely, *no one told me you were going.* The moment she thought this, however, she knew it wasn't fair, for she *had* been invited. Zachary had asked her if she wanted to go along and she had declined. In any case, she'd been far too busy earlier to leave the clinic.

As though drawn against their will, she found her eyes moving from Leila's colorful, animated face to Zachary's broad, handsome one. She found his narrowed eyes steadily fixed on her.

"Well, possibly some other time Carrie will decide she'd like me to take her," Zachary said, in his full, soft voice. "It really is a spectacular flight, Carrie," he added in an even softer voice, his eyes still insistently meeting hers. "If you'd ever like to go, you have only to let me know."

"Thank you," Carrie murmured, dropping her eyes, feeling her cheeks grow even warmer.

"Well, for now," Leila said, in her cheerful, booming voice, "we're headed toward the coffee shop. If you haven't had dinner yet, why don't you join us?"

"Thank you but I have had dinner." Carrie glanced again at Leila, forcing out a quick smile. "But thank you anyway."

"Well, at least come along and have coffee with us," Matt said. "Please say you will."

In confusion Carrie glanced into Matt's thin, embarrassed young face, then she felt her eyes being drawn irresistibly again toward Zachary's. He stood about four feet in front of her, Leila pressed close against him, her arm still possessively wound through his.

"Yes, Carrie, won't you join us, please?" Zachary echoed Matt's words.

Smiling nervously, Carrie murmured, "Thank you, but no. I just had two cups of coffee with dinner, and a third one is out of the question, though I thank you anyway." Bowing her head in farewell, she turned and began walking quickly away, back toward her clinic.

She'd gone only a few steps when she heard a rapid stride following. Glancing around, she saw that Matt was hurrying after her. He fell into step beside her.

"I'm really not in the least hungry," he explained, "as I just told Zack and Leila, so if you don't mind—is it all right if I walk you home?"

Wishing she knew how to say no without sounding rude and unfriendly, Carrie reluctantly agreed, doing her best to smile.

They walked for a few minutes in silence, then Matt remarked, "Just about the worst thing about being up here in the Arctic, it seems to me, is not the weather—that's not really so bad—or the hard work, or even the food, the worst thing it seems to me is the loneliness, or, more specifically, the fact there's so little to do during your leisure hours. Like tonight, for instance. Here it is only about seven o'clock, with the sun still shining, and if we were almost anywhere else, in almost any city in the world, there'd be places to go, things to do."

Matt paused, clearing his throat, then went on determinedly, "For instance, given circumstances like this, I could suggest going to a movie, or a play, or a concert, or a dance. But up here there's just so darn little one can do!"

"Yes, that's true," Carrie murmured in agreement, feeling exceedingly uncomfortable. By now Zachary and Leila would have reached the coffee shop, were probably taking a table and deciding what they would have. She felt a slight chill run over her and nervously pushed her mittened hands deeper into the pockets of her parka.

Matt walked along silently at her side for a time. To Carrie's intense relief they arrived at the clinic before he'd said anything more, though he kept nervously clearing his throat. As she turned to say goodnight, however, he reached out a hand to touch her arm.

"So what I was thinking about, Dr. Carrie," he said, his thin face tense, "is that maybe some evening the four of us—Zack, Leila, you, and me—well, maybe we could fly down to Kotzebue for a little fun, to go to the movie there or maybe bowl a few games, just to break the monotony. Or maybe some weekend— well, maybe we could all fly down to Nome or over to Fairbanks and really enjoy a change of scene. So what do you think, would you be willing to?" he ended, his eyes nervously, beseechingly meeting hers. "I'm sure Zack would be game to go, and Leila too. And certainly I would," he added with a sudden broad smile.

With a soft little answering smile, Carrie touched his hand where it held her arm and gave it a friendly squeeze. "Thank you, Matt, I appreciate the thought but I really don't think so, thanks. While admittedly there isn't much in the way of night life around here, nevertheless I keep myself pretty busy, reading, writing letters to my fiance, things like that. So thank you but I really think not."

"Oh." Matt drew his hand back with a crestfallen look. Apparently he hadn't noticed, the day they'd met in the clinic, the diamond engagement ring she wore.

"Well—well, thanks anyway for letting me walk you home," he muttered in embarrassment, and the next moment he had turned on his heel and was striding away. Poor lonely guy, Carrie thought, and with a sigh swung around and walked up the clinic steps.

She saw Zachary again the following day, once more in the late afternoon. By five her last patient had left, she'd then cooked herself a light meal in her quarters, and decided to go out for an early evening stroll through the village. She had walked only about twenty feet from the clinic when she realized that a man walking rapidly toward her, still well over a hundred yards away, had to be Zachary. No other man in the area was as tall and broad as that, with such thick curly black hair.

Her pulse suddenly dipping, Carrie stopped walking. The last person she wanted to see right now, or any time, was Zachary! Feeling suddenly breathless, she asked herself whether she shouldn't turn immediately around and return to the clinic, then retire to her bedroom. If Zachary had the nerve to enter the building and pound again on her door, she could simply ignore him. If she continued walking forward, there was no way she could avoid him. Unless she swung around and retreated right now, she was lost.

Even as she told herself this, Carrie felt too frozen to move. Gulping in the fresh cold air, she stopped walking and stared straight ahead, at the tall, powerful figure approaching her so rapidly. Suddenly the man's eyes met hers, across the distance still between them, and Zachary lifted a hand, waving to her, at the same time calling out in a warm, friendly voice, "Well, hi, neighbor. Lovely day, isn't it?"

"Yes, yes, it is," Carrie murmured nervously in answer. There was still time, if she'd but swing around and run, to return to the clinic and rush into her private quarters. So—what was holding her here?

Carrie swung around, away from the figure bearing down so relentlessly on her, but her legs by then were trembling so badly it wasn't easy to make them move. She had gone only a few yards when Zachary caught up with her, his powerful hand reaching out to grab her arm and stop her. He stood before her, grinning boyishly down at her, his gleaming dark eyes laughing at her, and once again Carrie felt the full force of his all but overpowering vitality, which seemed to envelop her so strongly there was no escape.

"Hello," Zachary greeted her, in his deep soft voice. "I'm delighted to run across you like this. Were you planning a walk down through the village?"

"Well—yes and no," Carrie murmured, drawing her arm free of his hold, her pulse pounding furiously.

Zachary grinned, his gleaming eyes openly mocking her. "That's what you were planning—until you saw me. Then you decided that you simply had to return to the clinic, quite possibly to hide away in your bedroom. No matter. If you're free for a time, would you do me the very great kindness of showing me around Point Hope? Though I've been in this general area for several months, I've yet to take in the sights here in the village, which I understand are quite worth seeing." After a slight pause, his grin fading away, Zachary added, "Please, Carrie, would you? I'd appreciate it very much."

As his dark eyes caught on hers, the mockery in them fading away. Carrie felt her pulse all but burst. "But—but why don't you ask Leila?" she responded nervously. "She knows the village far better than I do, and surely is free this evening too."

Zachary didn't answer at once. Instead he stood looking gravely down at her, then at last said, "Because I asked you. Will you, Carrie?"

Carrie opened her mouth to say no, she couldn't possibly do as he asked, but somehow these words just wouldn't come. As she dropped her eyes, her pulse calmed down. Would it really be too distressing to her to show him around? As they would be out in public view, Zachary would scarcely dare act as outrageously as he had in the clinic, grabbing and kissing her, so— why not? Especially as it would give her an excellent opportunity to make it clear to him that, in love with another man, she had absolutely no personal interest in him.

"Well—all right, if you like," Carrie murmured at last, and with an immediate smile Zachary took hold of her arm again and swung her back around.

"Thank you," he said, and as they fell into step walking, he dropped hold of her arm.

Though Carrie had been in Point Hope less than two weeks herself, she had twice gone on the guided tour of the village offered the small tourist groups who occasionally flew in for an overnight stay during the summer. An elderly Eskimo, a man who worked part time in one of the two local shops, had been her guide, and hopefully she'd remember enough of what he'd said to be able to answer any questions Zachary might have. If not—well, she'd certainly not made the slightest pretense that she was a knowledgeable guide!

They walked along in silence for a time, then Carrie suggested they start by visiting the graveyard, which was located about a mile to the east of the main village buildings. It was a unique cemetery, completely encircled by several hundred eight-foot-tall whale jawbones, with many of the graves marked with white crosses while others were marked with various animal bones.

After their tour of the cemetery, Carrie led the way to the old sod iglu village, reciting, as best she could remember, the virtues of these old, now-abandoned dwellings. One of the old sod homes, however, was still occupied, and Carrie led Zachary to the whalebones that marked which one it was. A dog was staked beside it, and an electric wire was connected from a nearby pole to its roof.

Carrie led Zachary twice around the small round mound, with growing amusement at the puzzlement soon evident on his face. "All right," he finally demanded, "if this mound is someone's house, where in the devil is the door?"

Laughing, Carrie swung around and pointed to a second mound almost a city block away. "There's a doorway clear over there," she explained, "if you can believe it. That's where one goes in, but, as big as you are, you'd really have to crouch down to make it. Are you game?"

"If you are," Zachary responded, with an immediate grin. As their eyes met, Carrie felt happy excitement race through her. She did her best to fight it down, however, as she swung around and began walking, Zachary at her side, toward the mound with the doorway in it that she'd pointed out.

Once they'd reached the second mound, Carrie crouched down to go through the doorway first. Smooth flagstones led down to another little doorway, and this one opened upon a spacious passage lit by a light bulb, also by a little skylight. The passage was completely lined with ancient whalebones covered with mold. After they'd traversed the passage, they arrived at a third door, even smaller than the first two. Carrie, glancing around at Zachary with a smile, asked him how he was doing. Bent over almost double, Zachary, with a grin, said he was doing just fine.

"Well, in that case I'll go ahead and knock." Carrie did so, knocking quite persistently for several minutes, but there was no answer.

"Well, probably just as well," Carrie murmured as she and Zachary swung around and started back down the passageway. "The house is so small, just one tiny room, and crowded with so much furniture, you wouldn't have fit in anyway," which brought a bursting laugh out of Zachary. His laugh sent another unsettling wave of excitement racing through Carrie, which she again did her best to fight down and ignore.

Next they walked down into the underground, natural deep-freeze storage room where meat was kept, then Carrie led the way to the shoreline, to the whale feasting grounds. As they left there, Carrie said that that was about all she knew to show him and that it was time she was getting home.

Zachary walked with her back through the village.

He invited her to dinner, but when Carrie responded that she'd already eaten, he said nothing more. When they arrived back at the clinic, Zachary stopped at the foot of the steps.

"Well, I thank you, Carrie, very much," he said. "I enjoyed it thoroughly and hope you didn't find it too unpleasant. For now I won't take up any more of your time. Possibly I'll see you again sometime." With these words, and a grave little nod of his head, he turned and strode off—to go see Leila? As though that's any business of mine! Carrie scolded herself, and with a little shake of her head she turned and ran up the clinic steps.

A few days later, on Sunday, Zachary arrived in Point Hope mid-morning and intercepted Carrie as she was walking home from church. She'd noticed a small plane winging down toward the airstrip and had wondered, with a slightly racing pulse, whether it could possibly be Zachary. Within minutes he was running up to fall into step beside her as she walked toward the clinic.

"Hi, doctor, it's certainly a gorgeous morning, isn't it?" he greeted her. "A perfect day for a spin upstairs to view the magnificent wonders God has created in these parts. How about it, Carrie, will you let me take you up for a flight?"

As his words died away, he stood before her frowning down at her, his dark eyes searching hers.

Momentarily Carrie bit nervously at her lip, then she nodded in agreement. "Thank you, Zack, on a day like this that would be nice," she murmured somewhat dubiously.

"Great!" Zachary exclaimed, and taking hold of her arm he began guiding her out toward the airstrip.

"You—didn't bring Matt along?" Carrie asked rather anxiously, feeling instantly unsure about what she had gotten herself into.

"Nope," Zachary said. "And don't suggest inviting Leila because I don't want her along either. Just thee and me, winging it toward the heavens . . ." With a quick bursting laugh, Zachary pulled her quickly along toward where his plane waited.

Within minutes they were in the air, and Carrie felt her pulse quicken with how beautiful everything was. From the air it was fascinating, and somehow very moving, to see the long spit of land upon which Point Hope was situated, a narrow finger sticking out into the cold, gray Chukchi Sea, perched so hopefully, yet forlornly, all by itself down there, miles and miles of bleak, desolate tundra to the east, and the endless, cold, open sea on the west.

"Up here you get some idea of the incredible vastness of the state," Zachary remarked. "It's the only state in the entire union, it seems to me, that you can't really appreciate except from the air. Just as your friend Leila said, whereas down in the lower states in most places you pretty much need a car, up here what you really need is a plane.

"First we'll follow the coastline up to Barrow, the northernmost point of the state, then we'll head south from there to give you a peek at the Brooks Range of mountains. How does that sound?"

"Sounds fine," Carrie answered, relaxing, beginning to feel excited and happy.

The village of Barrow was about nine miles southwest of Point Barrow, and as Zachary flew low over it, Carrie was surprised at the size of the town. Zachary mentioned that there were about twenty-five hundred inhabitants.

"That makes it the largest Eskimo settlement in the United States," Zack informed her. "The growth is mainly due to the federal government, and the various departments they've established down there, a Bureau of Indian Affairs office, a United States Public Health Service hospital, and the Office of Naval Research's Arctic Research Laboratory."

As Zachary circled back around the town a second time, he pointed out to Carrie the buildings comprising the N.A.R.L., the Naval Arctic Research Laboratory, the only United States scientific station devoted entirely to basic research in the Arctic. Established in 1947 in a quonset hut, it had grown to the size of a small village, a cluster of quonset huts along with one permanent, modern building completed in 1968, with seven wings housing forty-one separate modern laboratories for performing every imaginable kind of research, inland, along the coast, out on the sea ice, or in the air.

"That lab even has a role in the Eskimo whale hunts," Zachary told her with a grin. "The first word that Point Hope gets, for instance, that a whale is approaching comes via radio from monitors set up by the N.A.R.L."

"Fascinating," Carrie murmured, meaning it, thoroughly enjoying herself.

Before long Zachary left the village of Barrow behind, heading south, and Carrie stared greedily down at the landscape. This area of Alaska, known as the north slope, was a vast lake-dotted plain that had once been below the sea. In spite of the numerous lakes and ponds and the generally marshy nature of the area in summer, it was technically a desert, Zachary told her, having only four to five inches of rainfall a year. What kept it from being a *dry* desert, Zachary went on, was the layer of permafrost, the permanently frozen ground just a few inches below the surface. No water could drain through this, which allowed what little vegetation there was, the layer of tundra lichen and mosses such as Carrie was familiar with at Point Hope.

Before long Zachary gained altitude as they approached the Brooks Range, a mountain system which stretched, Zachary told her, six hundred miles from the Canadian border on the east to the Arctic Ocean on the west. Here too there was so little precipitation, a meager eight to twelve inches per year, that plant growth was nearly nonexistent, resulting in barren, treeless, desolate slopes.

As Carrie stared down, awed by the sight of the ruggedly beautiful mountain peaks, she began to feel rather frightened and chilled. A shiver ran through her. The mountain range, which separated the interior plain of Alaska from the Arctic or northern slope, seemed to stretch in every direction as far as the eye could see, one desolate, treeless slope giving way to another, then another, like one bleak, frightening summit mirrored through eternity. With a second little shiver she turned to face Zachary, ready to ask him please to turn back. But as though reading her mind he nodded, and swung them around.

On the way home they stopped at Zachary's work camp, four quonset huts ringed by a dozen sod houses. They had dinner there, then on to Point Hope.

As they set down on the airstrip, Carrie felt tired but happy. Zachary tried to hold her hand as they walked to the clinic, but when Carrie drew it free he made no further attempt to touch her.

Reaching the clinic steps, Carrie turned to say goodbye. "Zack, I really and truly enjoyed myself. Thank you for a very lovely day."

"I had a wonderful time too," Zachary said, "for which I thank you."

He bowed his head slightly, unsmiling, then turned and walked off.

CHAPTER
4

The long Arctic day finally drew to a close, the sun sinking briefly, palely, below the horizon once again.

After the day on which they'd taken the long scenic flight, Carrie didn't see Zachary again for over a month. For the first few days she found herself continually wondering what had happened. Possibly it had offended Zachary when she'd drawn her hand free of his as he was walking her toward the clinic. Or possibly he'd expected her to invite him inside upon their return and had gotten angry because she hadn't.

Was he still coming into the village? Rather than coming to see her, was he pursuing Leila now? Or had he found amusement somewhere else?

A week after their flight, Matt Sanders came limping into the clinic one morning with a badly sprained ankle, and while Carrie was treating him he happened to mention that Zachary was currently out of the area, having flown to Anchorage on business, and that he wouldn't be back for another three to four weeks, a simple explanation as to why Carrie hadn't seen him.

Summer wore on, gradually giving way to fall. The topsoil iced over and the snowfalls began. Carrie's days were busy and satisfying, her evenings, for the most part, long, restless, and boring. While she occasionally spent an hour or two with Leila, they were not really congenial and never became close friends. Though Zachary was surely back in the general area by then, Carrie never saw him, he never came to Point Hope. Though she often wondered if Leila was seeing him, she felt too embarrassed to ask, and kept reminding herself that it most certainly was no business of hers.

Then early one evening she returned to the clinic feeling wonderfully elated. With the aid of the village midwife, a wise, gentle, old Eskimo woman, she'd just delivered her first village baby, a beautiful, healthy boy, and she'd rarely felt so pleased with herself, or with life.

After she'd run up the clinic steps and stepped into the waiting room of the clinic, her heart bursting with good feelings, she saw to her surprise—and delight —that someone was there, sitting on the chair in front of the wooden table, and that someone was Zachary.

"Well, hello!" Carrie exclaimed, too happy not to show it, her face wreathed instantly in smiles. "This is a surprise!"

Grinning, Zachary rose to his feet, his dark eyes gleaming across at her. "God, but you're a sight for sore eyes," he said. "Even more beautiful than I remembered you. After the weeks I've just spent down in Anchorage wrangling with the bureaucrats—" He shook his head slightly, scowling, then grinned again. "So did you miss me?" he asked in a teasing tone.

Her pulse skipping excitedly, Carrie answered, in a

teasing tone to match his, "Oh, yes, excruciatingly. And when did you get back?" she added, walking toward the table as she drew off her parka.

"Early this morning." Zachary drew a Thermos bottle out of his jacket pocket, setting it down on the table top. "So how about having a drink with me, to celebrate? Hot chocolate made from an old family recipe kept secret for generations, better than any hot chocolate you've ever tasted."

"And what are we celebrating?" Carrie asked gaily. She sank down on the chair behind the table and glanced rather flirtatiously across, still grinning irresistibly at how happy she felt. "You know what I've just done?" she threw in impulsively. "I've just delivered my first village baby, a beautiful, healthy boy. If that's what you're suggesting we celebrate—"

"Naturally," Zachary said, his grin fading away as he uncapped the Thermos and poured steaming hot chocolate into the Thermos cup. "Of course, that's it." He drew out a second Thermos from his other pocket, unscrewed the top of that, and poured a second cupful, handing Carrie one. "So here's to the lovely baby," he said. "Cheers."

"Which you didn't even know about," Carrie said, with a nervous little giggle; then as she began sipping the chocolate, which in truth was delicious, her smile faded away. An awkward constraint seemed to fall upon them, and they sat for a time in silence sipping their drinks.

"Zack," Carrie asked at length, "how do you feel about children? Do you plan to have any when you marry?" An odd mist came into her eyes as she glanced across at him after asking this.

"Why of course I do!" Zachary exclaimed, sounding not only surprised but somewhat affronted. "You're damn right I do. Eight, ten, twelve, the more the merrier. What about you?"

Flushing, dropping her eyes, Carrie deliberately ignored the question, unwilling to admit to this vital, magnetic, thoroughly upsetting man that she and her fiance Mark had already decided they would never have any.

"But—but for heaven's sake, Zack," she responded instead, moving her eyes back to meet his, "surely you've heard of the population explosion? The human race is going to crowd itself right off the earth, or starve itself to death, if we don't stop multiplying so fast, and I don't care how much money or power you have, I don't think that gives you the right to have a family that size. Surely each of us owes it to everyone else to restrain himself!"

"Okay, you win," Zachary agreed with a shrug, his dark eyes steadily meeting hers. "So I'll only have one or two, then my wife and I will adopt the rest, give homes to kids who need one and don't have one. How's that?"

Carrie's eyes were caught on his, unable to move away, and for a moment her heart seemed almost to stop. But a second later, a slight shiver running down her frame, she managed to lower her eyes and sip her hot chocolate again, all her earlier elation dying away. Instead of feeling warm and happy, she began to feel sad and oddly chilled. When Zachary, apparently sensing her switch in mood, reached across to put his hand gently on top of hers, she allowed it for a moment, then with a tense smile drew her hand away, lifting both hands to hold her cup.

Though Zachary stayed for another half hour, she did not again feel at ease with him, or happy, and soon began wishing that he would leave. It had been a long, tiring day, and it took too much effort trying to be sociable with a man who invariably upset her.

That early evening visit of Zachary's was only the first of many such visits. By the middle of October Carrie had grown used to having him drop in four or five times a week, and had gotten to where she depended on him for company. When he stayed away more than two nights in a row, she would begin to feel restless and ill at ease. A couple of times a week he'd arrive early enough to take her to dinner at the village coffee shop, other times he'd show up a little later with his two Thermos bottles, sometimes filled with the thick, hot chocolate, other times with coffee, occasionally with a delicious, honey-laced tea. He'd pour them each a cupful, and in the tiny waiting room, while he sat on a chair in front of the table and she sat on Irvana's chair behind the table, they'd sit and talk.

On his second drop-in visit, Carrie brought up her fiancé's name so repeatedly, pointedly reminding Zachary of her engagement to another man, that from then on almost every visit Zack would ask her about Mark, whether he was still in Washington, D.C., still working to promote the Wilderness Areas Bill. Zachary seemed now to accept, without a trace of rancor, that she was in love with another man and fully intended to marry him. Apparently any romantic feeling he'd ever had for her had now died away, or been repressed, and his only interest now was in whiling away a pleasant hour with her once in a while. A couple of times Carrie had dared to suggest that possibly he should be spending his spare time visiting Leila rather than her, but Zachary had turned the suggestion aside, commenting that he preferred Carrie's company, which even Leila had good naturedly accepted by then. And as long as he behaved himself, didn't act up again as he had earlier, Carrie had to admit she enjoyed seeing him.

Although Zachary frequently asked her about Mark, and they occasionally got into brief discussions about energy needs versus environmental protection, Carrie instinctively drew back from lengthy arguments, always doing her best to steer the conversation away from touchy areas. She knew from the comments that Zachary made that he was as confirmed a believer in what he was doing as she was in what Mark was doing, so with such widely divergent beliefs, there was no hope of any compromise. In her heart she still looked upon Zachary as a man she could never respect, a man amassing a huge fortune through his ruthless exploitation—his uncaring rape—of the earth, a man who had eagerly joined the committee formed to defeat the Wilderness Areas Bill, the very thing she and Mark most strongly believed in. But as she had clearly stated how she felt about him long before now, back when they'd first met, she could see little point in throwing her scorn and disrespect into his face again, and possibly getting drawn into an ugly fight about it.

On frequent occasions Zachary, baiting her, tossed at her good-natured comments supporting his own views and opposing hers, trying to draw answering comments from her. But, after listening tensely to what he had to say, Carrie would resolutely turn the conversation aside, so determined was she not to get drawn into useless argument with him.

One night as Zachary was leaving, after they'd spent a very pleasant two hours talking together, he put out his hand to her, grinning, the first time in weeks he'd made any attempt to touch her. Standing behind the table, Carrie, with a slightly nervous smile, slipped her own thin hand into his large one.

"Friends now, right?" Zachary challenged her, his dark eyes warmly enveloping her.

Carrie could feel her cheeks flush, could feel her pulse give a little leap. After biting momentarily at her lip, she glanced up to murmur in answer, "Well— friendly enemies anyway," for surely that was the best they could ever hope to achieve, so disparate were their views.

"Well, all right," Zachary said, dropping her hand with a sigh. "Good-night then, beloved enemy." Leaning over he kissed her very briefly on the cheek, taking her completely by surprise, before he turned and strode out.

He didn't return again for two weeks, by which time Carrie had begun to feel certain she would never see him again. November crept in, icily cold, and late one afternoon a howling blizzard blew up, immobilizing the village, reducing visibility to zero. Fortunately the villagers had had sufficient forewarning to take the few precautions possible. Two days before, in expectation of the foul weather due, ropes had been strung from building to building in the tiny settlement so that those few hardy souls who had to venture out could find their way and not become hopelessly lost when the blinding storm struck.

Isolated in her sturdy little building with her stove belching out enough heat to keep her warm, Carrie sat at the little table in the tiny waiting room bent over a medical book. For the first time in weeks she felt swept through with loneliness, almost paralyzed by it. In trying to combat it, she had done her best to turn her thoughts happily to Mark, bringing out a small bundle of his letters hoping to find solace in rereading them, but it hadn't worked. Though she had struggled through four or five of them, she had felt too bored after that to go on. Next she tried to concentrate on a medical text, hoping in that way to ease the wrenching pain of isolation she felt.

Suddenly someone pushed the door open and stepped quickly inside, forcefully shaking his head and body to throw off the snow and sleet that all but covered him.

"Zack!" Carrie cried in surprise, jumping up, unable to hide the delight she felt even from herself. The one person on earth she had most hoped to see . . .

Zachary, remaining by the door, brushed himself off a bit more, his broad handsome face grinning across at her. As Carrie stepped excitedly forward to greet him, he strode forward too, arms lifting as though to grab her to him.

"God, you look beautiful when you're excited!" he said, bearing down upon her, his exuberant vitality such a living force it seemed to reach Carrie and wrap her up tightly even before Zachary could.

"Don't please," she whispered in answer, hurriedly backing off. "Don't spoil it, please. Naturally I'm happy to see you but try to understand."

By then she had sidestepped her way back behind the table, where she dared to face him again, looking at him beseechingly. "For hours I've been here all alone, ever since noon when I sent Irvana home, all alone listening to that wretched blizzard outside, not knowing how many hours, how many days even, I might be shut up here all by myself.

"Don't you see," she suddenly pleaded, pulse pounding hard, "under those circumstances I'd be delighted to see anyone, anyone at all, even the devil himself. But that doesn't mean—"

Her voice died away through her pulse kept hammering, sending excited blood spilling furiously through her veins. To be cut off from everyone else in the world, with only Zachary here . . . Her body was abruptly seized by a frenzied trembling that she didn't seem able to control, so she quickly sank down on the chair behind the table to attempt to hide the nervous state she was in.

"So please, Zack," she pleaded again, voice shaking, sharp, needlelike pains stabbing through her head, "it *is* nice to see you . . ."

"Even though I'm the devil himself," Zachary muttered, his broad grin fading into a wry smile. "Well, that agreed upon, let's settle down and warm ourselves up a bit. I've brought along my Thermos bottles, naturally."

He pulled a quart Thermos out of each pocket of his parka, set them both down on the table, threw back his parka hood to reveal his gleaming black hair, and unscrewed the cap of each Thermos to give them two cups from which to drink. "Hot buttered rum, nothing better in weather like this." He pushed one of the cups across the table toward Carrie, saying with mock sternness, "So drink up, my lady. If anything can warm your heart, this will."

With a small, uncertain smile, Carrie picked up the cup he had filled for her and began to sip. How hot and delicious the drink was! As Zachary smiled warmly across at her, sipping from his own cup, Carrie lowered her eyes and sipped some more, trying to control a sudden trembling in her arms. Was it wise for her to drink even one small cup of such a potent drink? Was Zachary playing some wily cat-and-mouse game with her, hoping to catch her a little off guard—a little intoxicated perhaps—so he could pounce?

As she stared down at the rough table top sipping cautiously at her drink, Carrie could feel unbidden tears rise into her eyes, and she half wished that Zachary hadn't come, that she could go back to feeling dreadfully lonely—and safe. The storm within her now seemed almost to match the howling blizzard outside.

"Don't be afraid of me, Carrie, please," Zachary said suddenly, softly, one of his hands reaching across to gently touch hers. As Carrie's eyes jerked up—how was it he could so often read her mind?—he went on, in the same soft voice, "I give you my word right now, my solemn promise, that I will never force you in any way. I'm in love with you, have been, in truth, from the very first day, but until such time as you feel the same—" Instead of finishing the sentence, he gave a little shrug, his lips curling in a sweet, sad smile. "So drink up, doctor, okay? I only brought it along to warm you up, not to mess you up in any way, all right?"

With an encouraging grin, Zachary lifted his cup in a toast, and Carrie, relaxing, lifted her cup in an answering toast and they both took long deep swallows of the bracing hot drink.

When they finished their first small cupfuls, Zachary poured them a second, and they were half way through those when the clinic door was again pushed open, to Carrie's amazement, and a young Eskimo, Niago, the husband of her pregnant patient, Niksaaktug, stepped hurriedly inside, almost blown down by the force of the freezing wind before he successfully got the door closed again.

"Niago, what is it?" Carrie cried in immediate alarm, jumping up. "Is Niksaaktug? . . ." her first thought being that Niago must have braved the storm to come fetch her to attend to his wife. But she had seen Niksaaktug that very morning, around eleven, and everything had seemed to be fine. Hurrying forward, Carrie went on in extreme agitation, "Is it your wife, Niago? Has something happened? Does she need me? Is that why you came?"

Suddenly she became aware of strong hands gripping her shoulders, holding her back. "Easy there, Carrie, easy," Zachary murmured. "Getting into a stew isn't going to help anyone." After flashing her a soft, calming smile, Zachary turned to Niago. "What's the problem, friend? Why have you come?"

"Niksaaktug," the young man gasped out, his dark eyes filled with fear as he looked from Carrie to Zachary and back again to Carrie. He stood just inside the door, his form almost lost in the snow and ice that clung to his bulky clothing. The owner-proprietor of one of the two village stores, with a curio and souvenir section which catered to tourists in season, he had a good command of the English language. "My wife isn't here?" he cried out, in an anguished voice. "She didn't come see you today, Dr. Carrie?"

"Yes, yes, she did," Carrie responded, fear making her feel icy cold suddenly. "But she left here long before noon, Niago, hours and hours ago. Hasn't she returned home?"

Niago shook his head, even greater despair coming into his eyes. He lifted an arm to press it against his nose, looking momentarily unable to speak again.

"Well, but—maybe she went to the store," Carrie suggested, her pulse now pounding. "Have you tried there? Surely she's all right, what could have happened to her? The blizzard didn't even blow up until one, she'd been gone for over an hour by then. Are you sure she isn't at the store?" Carrie asked again, in growing panic.

"No, no, I went there hours ago," Niago muttered. "She didn't come home, didn't go to the store . . ." A sob escaped him, then he turned away, his hand out to grab the doorknob as though he meant to leave again.

Zachary stepped quickly past Carrie and his hand shot out to grab Niago's arm. "Hey, hold on, friend," he said. "There's no point in going racing out there until we at least try to figure out where your wife might have gone. With the ropes already strung up all through the village, even if the blizzard blew up before she got home, she would have been able to make it to the store. So if she didn't go there—get him a cup of that drink, would you, Carrie?" Zachary suddenly threw in.

Glad to be doing something, no matter of how little help it might be, Carrie hurried back to the table, picked up the cup she'd been using, filled it quickly with hot buttered rum, then she cradled the hot cup in her hands and carried it forward to where Niago stood, offering it to him. With a little nod, Niago took the cup from her and drank down several mouthfuls. As he lowered the cup again, he said, "My wife's brother arrived in the village a few days ago. He's built himself a snowhouse over that way." Niago motioned toward the northeast. Shaking his head, he added despairingly, "But surely she wouldn't have gone away from the village to visit him. If she left the village to go visit him . . ." His voice broke as he again pressed his arm furiously against his nose.

Carrie looked hopelessly over at Zachary, sick inside

with the certainty that that must have been what Niksaaktug had done. Assuming she had, if she'd left her brother's snowhouse again before the blizzard struck, expecting to get safely back to the village before the storm began, only to get caught in it instead . . . Within minutes, once the blizzard swooped down, she could have been so completely lost, so blinded by the swirling ice and snow, that she could have traveled around in circles for hours, within a few yards of her destination, of her salvation, yet never reaching it, dropping down finally in complete exhaustion, never to rise again, freezing to death right there.

Shuddering with fear, Carrie glanced over hoping to catch Zachary's eyes, to gain comfort from his strength, also to share with him the keen, stabbing sorrow she felt.

But to her distress she saw that the farthest thing from Zachary's mind was offering comfort to her. Rather, his dark eyes gleaming with determination, he drew the hood of his parka up over his head, then his large hand clamped down on Niago's shoulder.

"Your wife must have gone to her brother's," Zachary said in a firm voice which somehow contained great tenderness in it. "Quite possibly she is safe there, or if not, if she started back and got caught in the blizzard . . . Come on, I'll help you search for her."

"Zack, no!"

The cry, wrenched from deep within her being, burst out of Carrie before she even knew she meant to protest. Eyes blinded by tears, she rushed forward to catch Zachary's arm, grabbing hold of the thick sleeve of his parka, wishing she could grab his bare flesh, dig her nails deep into his flesh to stop him.

"Zachary, no!" she cried again. "Zack, that's suicide, you'll never find her. I grew up in this state, all my life I've heard of blizzards like this, of people lost within minutes of venturing out, going round and round in circles only yards away from safety. There's no way at all you can find her, you'd only be throwing your own life away!"

Zachary's dark green eyes, narrowing, gazed steadily down on her, then with his free hand he freed the grip of her hand on his arm. "Nonsense," he said, with a broad boyish grin, his handsome face flushed. "We'll be all right."

As Carrie, sick with fright, backed a step from him, biting her lip to keep from crying, Zachary stepped forward toward her, catching hold of her by both arms.

"But just in case you're right," he murmured, his grin dying away, "there's one thing I must have . . ." And the next moment he swept her close against him, holding her so tightly in his powerful arms she felt faint from breathlessness, and his mouth came down on hers, hard, forceful, seeking, demanding, a kiss such as Carrie had never experienced before, one in which the mouth passionately possessing hers seemed to be drawing out of her her very soul, leaving nothing in her untouched, nothing unprofaned.

Oh, God, please! Carrie thought wildly, but still Zachary's mouth held hers captive, still it moved hotly, forcefully, on hers, possessing her ever more completely. Weak in the knees, tremors running up and down her arms, Carrie could feel herself melting against him, melting—and then abruptly the kiss ended, Zachary thrust her back from him. He swung away, pulled the door open and was gone, head down as he stepped out into the swirling, blinding, killing storm, Niago following after him, yanking the door reclosed.

Carrie ran quickly to the door, reopened it, and stepping through it, snow and ice immediately slashing furiously into her face.

"Zack, no, don't go!" she cried, yelling the words with all her might, knowing the sound wouldn't carry a foot. In the fury of the storm the human voice was drowned. Though she had followed the two men as quickly as she could move, yanking the door back open barely seconds after Niago had pulled it closed, they were already lost to sight. Visibility was nonexistent. There was only the violent, slashing wind, whirling everything before it, carrying sure death in its wake.

"Oh, no, Zack, why did you go?" Carrie moaned, and then with a shudder she turned back and reentered the clinic. She walked across the tiny waiting room, sat down behind the desk, drew over the cup from which Zachary had been drinking, and thoughtlessly drank down what it contained. This was the last clear memory she had. After that she really couldn't remember anything.

Except for the waiting, and the excruciatingly slow pulse of time. No matter how infrequently she looked at her watch, the minute hand never seemed to have moved at all, and the only reality was the deep sorrow and despair she felt. Lovely young Niksaaktug, chosen Queen of the Village in July, soon thereafter marrying the handsome young Niago, so quietly, radiantly happy to be bearing his child, lost now somewhere out in the blizzard, her frantic young husband venturing out in a hopeless search for her, and Zachary . . .

Oh, Zack, it just wasn't sensible to do that, Carrie thought, her mind caught up in its own whirling kind of numbing, freezing storm. What good will it do poor, sweet Niksaaktug to have you and Niago die too? What a waste, what a terrible, mind-blowing waste!

But she'd done her best to warn them, to stop them, what more could she possibly have done?

In time she rose from her chair, picked up one of the Thermos bottles Zachary had brought, and poured herself a fresh cup of buttered rum. She had all but drunk it down, a thoughtless sip at a time, when the waiting-room door was suddenly pushed open and Zachary came loping into the room, a limp, snow-coated bundle in his arms, followed by Niago, who quickly reclosed the door, shutting out the violent, deafening storm.

"Oh, my God," Carrie cried, jumping up, "I can't believe it—you found her! Is she—?" She couldn't complete the question, she could only leave it hanging there as she rushed forward to meet the returning men.

Stepping past her without breaking stride, Zachary said, his broad face breaking into a joyful, triumphant grin, "Pure dumb luck, that's all it was. But she's still breathing, her pulse seems strong." Saying no more, he managed to lean down to turn the knob on the inner door, and after kicking it open he went into the treatment room and placed his snow-laden burden down on the sheet-covered treatment table.

Her pulse jumped wildly, joy nearly bursting in her heart. Carrie thought, *Oh, Zack, I could kiss you, I could smother you with kisses!* but without speaking to him, without even glancing his way again, she hurried into the treatment room after him, and the moment he had placed Niksaaktug onto the table she caught up the young woman's wrist, checking the pulse, and bent her head down against her chest. Just as Zachary had said, Niksaaktug—thankfully!—*was* still breathing, her pulse *was* strong. Thank God, Carrie thought, and set about unzipping Niksaaktug's

- 71 -

parka, ready to begin administering to her patient, to bring her back to consciousness.

And though she did not speak, or even look around at the two men for quite some time, in spite of herself Carrie kept thinking, her heart bursting with it, *Oh, Zack, you darling, you great big darling, I could kiss you, kiss you, kiss you for this!*

But this was just a figure of speech, Carrie kept assuring herself as she worked happily over her rescued patient; she did not mean it literally. Certainly not.

CHAPTER 5

Just as Irvana stepped out on the clinic porch followed by Carrie, the sled drew up, the lead dog, a gleaming white Siberian husky, panting for breath, his intelligent eyes glancing immediately around toward his master.

A stout, middle-aged Eskimo man, his face all but hidden behind the fur-lined hood of his parka, hurried up to the foot of the steps and began pouring out his story to Irvana, speaking so rapidly, in what Carrie knew was a back-country dialect, that she caught not a word of it. Even Irvana seemed to be having some difficulty in understanding, for she repeatedly questioned the man in a rather sharp voice, until at last she seemed satisfied that she had understood what he was saying.

"Dr. Carrie," Irvana relayed the message, "at the camp where they are, a party of about thirty, he says, one of the men has fallen very ill. High fever, abdominal cramps. He was in such pain they were afraid to bring him here, and he says they have heard that sometimes you are kind enough to leave your home and go visit the sick people where they are, and they beseech you to do this very great kindness for them."

As Irvana gave Carrie this message, the Eskimo, standing at the foot of the steps, kept his great dark eyes fastened anxiously on her. If one of the men in the camp had fallen seriously ill . . .

"Tell him of course I'll come," Carrie answered at once, offering the man a nod before turning around to step back inside the clinic. "I'll get my bag and be right with him." She walked hurriedly, purposefully, across the tiny waiting room and into her treatment room, trying hard not to despair over this sudden, unexpected development. Of all the days she did not want to be called away . . .

This was the last week of November, and she hadn't seen Zachary since the night he had so gallantly gone out into the blizzard in search of Niksaaktug. After the young woman had regained consciousness that night and Carrie had done all she could to minimize the effects of the exposure she had suffered, she had told Niago that she didn't want her patient taken out into the cold; she wanted her to spend the night right where she was, warmly bundled up. Carrie had added that of course Niago was welcome to stay overnight too, if he wished, though she had no bed to offer him. With a shy smile Niago had accepted the invitation, saying that he'd be fine curled up on the floor. Carrie and Zachary had then stepped out into the tiny waiting room to share a private word of good-bye.

Carrie had still felt terribly unsettled about the evening's happenings: Zachary's passionately possessive kiss before he'd ventured out into the blizzard, her fear that he might never return, the exultation she'd felt when he had not only returned but, with Niago, had found Niksaaktug and saved her life.

She had felt awkward when she was alone again with him, her cheeks flushing with the thought that she wished she could think of some proper way to thank him, without having him interpret any gesture she made as more personal than it was. She knew she had to be extremely careful, for hadn't he, this very evening, declared himself to be in love with her? As she was not in the slightest degree in love with him, merely felt grateful to him, how could she express this without having him read more into her words than she meant, especially if she followed her deepest impulse to reach up, after thanking him, to press a loving kiss on his cheek? No, he would misinterpret everything she said, everything she did, might all too quickly grab her close again and force another passionate, lover's kiss upon her, the very thing she least wanted, in fact would not tolerate again. Therefore she *must* restrain herself and not express any warm feelings she had, for which restraint Zachary had only himself to blame!

Deciding this, Carrie said, in a light, easy tone, "Well, friend, shall we finish off the little bit of buttered rum that's still left? Incidentally," she added, blushing again in spite of herself, her gray eyes dropping, "just as I felt it was a poor idea for Niago to venture out again in this storm, the same holds true for you. I don't have a spare bed to offer you, unfortunately, but if you were to draw some chairs together—" she made a nervous gesture with her hands, "I do have extra bedding, and no matter how uncomfortable that is, it would surely be better than having to go out into that dreadful blizzard again."

She felt not the least concern making this offer, for after all between this small room and the door into her living quarters was the treatment room, wherein both Niksaaktug and Niago would be sleeping. Even Zachary, with his reckless zest for going after what he wanted, would never dare accost her under such circumstances. Therefore he was most certainly welcome to bed down here.

"Thank you, dear friend," Zachary answered lightly, grinning. Grabbing up a Thermos, he poured out what was left of the buttered rum into one of the cups. He handed the cup to Carrie, then swooped up his second Thermos, already empty and recapped, slid that into one of his pockets, and patiently waited, with a friendly smile, while Carrie sipped from the cup.

A moment later, blushing, Carrie handed the cup from which she'd been drinking to Zachary, murmuring, "There, I've had my share, the rest is yours." Zachary, dark green eyes gleaming down at her, took the cup and finished it off, his glance never leaving her face. A moment later he recapped the second Thermos, slid it into his other pocket, then pulled his hood up over his head, swinging around toward the door, saying, "Well, good-night, friend."

Carrie stepped quickly after him, protesting, "But—aren't you going to stay here? Why not, for heaven's sake? To go out into that storm again—where will you sleep?" She shivered suddenly, uncontrollably, at the mere thought of his leaving this way, and her eyes fastened anxiously on his face as he glanced back, still smiling softly, to answer her.

"Thank you, sweet Carrie, but I really have to be leaving. I can hang onto the ropes and will do just fine. Thanks anyway."

The next moment, to her surprise, he swung back,

took a long step toward her, grabbed her by the arms, and half lifting her from the floor drew her up to kiss her, a hotly possessive kiss that again seemed to draw out every part of her, to leave no portion of her being unpossessed, unmolested. Tears of anger, of terrible outrage, rose to her eyes before he finally let her loose and, swinging away, was quickly gone, exiting through the door which he carefully pulled shut after himself.

Her stinging eyes threatening to overflow, Carrie thought despairingly, *After he promised he would never force himself on me; this very night he promised he wouldn't—just see how much his word is worth!* How could she ever truly trust him?

Retiring to her bedroom, she changed into warm nightclothes, then crawled into bed, only to find she was too keyed up to sleep. The memory of Zachary's kisses—the long rapacious one before he'd headed out into the blizzard, the equally passionate one he'd forced upon her just before leaving—burned too hotly within her. The man was impossible. She should have known better than to let her guard down even the little she had. Just as he had piled up an enormous fortune circling the globe, raping and plundering the earth of all its hidden resources, if she gave in to his kisses he would do the same to her, exploit and plunder and exhaust her, leaving nothing of her in existence when, having had his fill of her, he moved on from her to exploit and plunder someone new.

Tears burned hotly in her eyes, and Carrie trembled with the insistent memory of his kisses while her mind raged against him, against the kind of man he was and the way he was treating her. Was there no defense against his ruthless determination to pillage and destroy her?

After an almost sleepless night of endless tossing, Carrie climbed out of bed in the morning with a firm resolve. The very next time she saw Zachary she would tell him that she had changed her mind and that they were no longer even friendly enemies. How could true enemies ever be friendly? She would also tell him that while she did not hold against him his frequent friendly visits, which admittedly she had enjoyed, she wished them now to cease. If he challenged her on this, demanding to know why, she would tell him straightforwardly, making no attempt whatsoever to spare his feelings. Once too often he had grabbed her, kissing her against her wishes, and she wasn't willing to risk having it happen ever again.

With this determination Carrie faced the new day, with the blizzard still howling outside. As soon as she had washed and dressed, she hurried into the treatment room to check on her patient, and found the young woman awake and cheerful. At her first glimpse of Niksaaktug's brightly attractive young face, Carrie felt another wave of warm gratitude toward Zachary, but she quickly stamped out this positive feeling toward him, telling herself she must not be tempted to weaken toward him again. The very next time she saw him . . .

But he didn't drop by that day, nor the next, nor the one after that. After these days of not seeing him, it became harder and harder to stay steeled up and determined; a growing loneliness for him grew like an unwelcome cancer within her. She'd grown so used to seeing him—where was he anyway? The last she'd seen of him he'd grabbed her, forced a kiss upon her, then headed out into the howling blizzard. How typical of him not even to let her know he'd survived the storm and was perfectly all right!

But of course he was all right, Carrie kept telling herself in annoyance; she wasn't really worried that anything had happened to him. This was just further proof of his thoughtlessness, that was all.

Then five days after she'd last seen Zack, Matt Sanders dropped by the clinic. Looking embarrassed, he told her that Zachary had sent him with the message that he'd been called away on business to the lower states but hoped to get back to Point Hope by the end of the month, and he would drop by to see her then.

In spite of herself Carrie felt instant relief pour through her. So that was it; Zack had been called away, and wouldn't be back until the end of the month. The moment he came to see her then, she would, of course, give him the word that she did not wish to see him ever again.

But now the time had passed, the endless three weeks, and Zack would surely be back. This was the thirtieth, the last day of the month. If he was going to make it back by the month's end, today was it. Carrie had felt tense and keyed up since waking that morning, so certain had she felt that Zachary would be over to see her that day. But so far he hadn't come, and now the dogsled had pulled up, the stout, anxious-eyed Eskimo having come all the way from his camp to plead with her to return with him, and of course she had no choice but to do so, no choice at all.

Carefully filling her medical bag with those supplies she might need, Carrie did her best to suppress her deep sighs, and within a brief time she had the bag filled. She zippered it up, then resolutely left her treatment room, crossed the tiny waiting room, and stepped out onto the small porch. After nodding good-bye to Irvana, she hurried down the steps and walked back to take her place in the sled. If Zachary *did* come this evening . . . Oh, well, she had no choice but to go with this man and render aid.

With grateful black eyes, the Eskimo helped her down into the sled, which he had already swung around into the right direction. But then, just as he called out his first clear command to the lead dog, Carrie heard the sound she'd been waiting to hear all day—Zachary's firm, quick stride. Glancing instantly around, cheeks flushing, pulse pounding, she saw it was indeed Zack, rapidly approaching the clinic. Then, as their eyes met, as he saw her there in the sled, he broke into a run toward where she sat.

"Wait, wait!" Carrie cried hurriedly to the Eskimo, then in confusion she repeated the words in Eskimo. Almost before she'd gotten the words out, Zachary was there, his large strong hands pulling her up. Without a word of greeting, he quickly lowered himself into the sled, pulled Carrie down to sit in front of him, spread the lap furs over them both, then nodded to the Eskimo that they were now all set. Without invitation or even one question he was going along! Isn't that just like him, Carrie thought. While she tried to think it indignantly, a pleased smile spread irrepressibly across her face as the Eskimo again called to his lead dog and the sled started sliding smoothly forward.

Nestling down into Zachary's arms, Carrie closed her eyes and gave herself up to the pleasure of his nearness. If only he could always be like this, simply near her, his arms around her to hold and protect her, not to grab her and force her to him! In this position she didn't have to face him, to look into those piercing eyes which continually made such passionate demands of her, just as his mouth made such insistent demands when it ruthlessly pressed down on hers. If only he would care about her, and take care of her, as he was doing now, without wanting more in return than she could possibly ever give him without completely destroying herself. With this thought Carrie sighed, feeling restless for the moment within the circle of Zachary's powerful, comforting arms. He hadn't said he loved her, rather he'd said he was *in* love with her, and what a world of difference that made!

With the sudden hurting restlessness in her heart, Carrie twisted her head around, yelling against the force of the cold wind which went whistling by them, "Well, Zack, how have you been?" her eyes not quite able to meet his.

But Zack responded with only the one word, "No!" shaking his head at her, and Carrie knew that he meant she wasn't to try to talk. Somehow his saying that soothed her into inner restfulness again, and turning back forward she snuggled down a bit deeper, feeling Zachary's arms tighten around her, and closing her eyes she let herself slip into a fantasy that from now on it would always be this way—Zachary, like a brother or loving friend, would be gentle and sweet with her from now on, understanding her needs and doing his best to fulfill them instead of so ruthlessly pursuing his own. Surely he knew by now that she wasn't in love with him, never could be, and that the only way they could continue seeing each other was if he adjusted himself to this and settled for being her very dear friend. How wonderful that would be, Carrie thought, and with a little sigh gave herself up to the comforting strength of his nearness.

They traveled for what seemed close to an hour, Carrie with her eyes closed, at times all but drifting off into sleep, then their forward motion ceased. Carrie opened her eyes, blinked hard a couple of times, and saw they had reached their destination, an Eskimo camp. A circle of snowhouses ringed them and several Eskimo men and women stood in front of their temporary homes watching the doctor arrive with shyly curious smiles.

"Well, here we are," Zachary murmured, and gave her one last, unnecessary squeeze. The Eskimo man who had come for her hurried alongside the sled to take her hand and help her up. The moment she was on her feet, bag in hand, the man gestured to one of the snowhouses and started toward it, motioning for her to follow.

Inside the small snowhouse, or iglu, a temporary shelter which had been built out of snowblocks by members of the hunting party, Carrie found her patient, a young male lying on a bed of furs. He offered her a grateful smile as she bent over him, and Carrie smiled back in reassurance. Placing her hand to his forehead, she found his skin was excessively warm, almost burning to the touch. His pulse raced, his respiration was rapid and shallow. She opened her bag and drew out instruments to make a more thorough examination.

Within forty minutes she had done all she knew how to do. Having diagnosed his illness as nothing more serious than an acute case of intestinal flu, she gave him a powerful antibiotic shot, rubbed him down gently with snow to bring his fever down as quickly as possible, and with gestures and the few words she knew of Eskimo got the message through to the man's wife that he should be given one of the pills she was leaving every three hours, also that he should be brought to the clinic to see her the following day, if he was well enough to travel, otherwise she would come see him again. Then she crawled out of the snowhouse again, feeling suddenly tired, more than ready to return home.

As she stood up, pulling her parka hood back into position over her head, Zachary neared her, grinning. Although it wasn't yet three o'clock by her watch, the last rays of the sun had already faded away, and the long Arctic night had begun.

"All set, doctor?" Zachary asked her, his dark eyes smiling warmly down at her. He took her arm, adding, "It must give you a good feeling to be able to help people this way, to allay their fears if nothing else. I'm proud of you, Carrie." He leaned down to press a kiss on her cheek, causing Carrie instantly to tense and draw slightly away. This brought an even broader grin to Zachary's face and then a brief laugh.

"Well, come on, Miss Touch-Me-Not," he said jovially. "We've been offered a dogsled to take us back to the village. Here you go." He helped her down into the sled, bundling her up with the lap furs, his gleaming eyes catching on hers for an instant. To Carrie's surprise, he threw her a pleased little wink, which caused her to tense. With another brief, amused laugh he took up his position behind the sled, took the control whip in hand, and after nodding his thanks to the Eskimo men of the small hunting camp, who stood around in a little circle seeing them off, Zachary called out to the lead dog and the sled eased forward. Bundling herself up even more warmly in the lap furs, Carrie sighed.

Feeling tired, she repeatedly closed her eyes, but couldn't seem to keep them closed. As close as Zachary was, riding the runners of the sled right over her head, he seemed very distant. How much nicer it had been on the trip out, having him right here with her, where she could rest against him and feel his strong arms around her! Blinking, feeling suddenly not only tired but depressed and lonely, Carrie thought back to their departure from the hunting camp, the way Zachary, apparently simply as a gesture of approval and appreciation, had leaned down to kiss her cheek. In spite of herself she had instantly tensed, drawing away, as though even a peck on the cheek—from him—was a gross affront.

Oh, dear, Carrie thought, and her distress increased. If only she knew herself how she felt about the man! But she never seemed able to sort out her feelings once and for all. If only she didn't feel this constant little nagging loneliness, if only she and Mark could be together . . .

Well, soon they would be, she consoled herself, lifting her chin a bit, and once she was with Mark again, could see him and embrace him, all this silly conflict that Zachary caused in her would be a thing of the past. She knew well enough what she wanted; she wanted Mark, wanted to live her life as his wife. They had known and loved each other for so long, shared the same beliefs, the same goals. Life with Mark would be precisely the kind of life she wanted, and she most certainly was not going to risk that life by allowing herself to feel drawn to Zack, a man who was undeniably physically magnetic. She felt more physically attracted to Zack, she had to admit, than she'd ever felt toward any man. But infatuation of that kind, no matter how powerful it was, wasn't love. All she had to consider was the kind of man Zachary was, and she wouldn't have the least problem resisting him, no matter with what wiles he tried to win her. Still—well, she still couldn't quite kill off her regret that he wasn't seated with her here in the sled, his powerful arms holding her close as she rested back against him. On the trip out his closeness had felt so good, so warmly comforting.

The dogs ran at a hard, steady pace. The sled moved smoothly over the snow, and before long, having again settled her mind about Zachary, Carrie reclosed her eyes, and this time she drifted off into a light sleep and dreamed that Zachary was with her in the sled, his arms around her, except that she was facing him, and his mouth was claiming hers in a long, soft kiss. She fell even more soundly asleep.

Zachary's voice woke her quite as much as his hand shaking her arm, or the beam of the flashlight he held. "Carrie. Carrie, wake up!" his voice said sharply. "Wake up, sweetheart."

Carrie's eyes popped open and she found herself staring straight into his eyes, which were only a few inches from hers, the beam of the flashlight he held illuminating his face.

"That's the girl," Zachary said, grinning. "A slight blizzard has blown up, as you can see if you'll look around, and I hate to admit it but I've gotten us lost. The fact is I don't know where the hell we are. For the last twenty minutes we've been going around in circles, I'm afraid. It seems to me the best thing to do is spend the night right here, then try to find our way back to Point Hope in the morning. What do you say?"

Her pulse gave an immediate, hard leap of excitement and fear. Carrie pulled up, glancing quickly around. Snow slashed against her face, and staring into the dark she could see that Zachary was telling the truth; a storm had blown up. Visibility was little more than a few feet; a howling wind made it difficult even to hear one's thoughts. Oh, dear God, Carrie thought, and wondered in fright whether they'd even survive the night.

"Give me your hand so I can pull you up," Zachary said. "I've got to get the tools stashed away there at your feet. Also I'll need your help." Grinning at her, he helped her up, and for a moment Carrie thought, from the look that flashed through his eyes, that he meant to grab her close and kiss her, but obviously she was wrong, for he did no such thing. Instead he bent over the sled, tossing the lap furs aside, directing the flashlight beam there, and a moment later he drew out a short-handled ax.

"Ah, here we are," he said. He leaned down again and this time drew out a long, sturdy rope. "Just as a precaution," he yelled at Carrie, encircling her waist with it and tying it, then pulling it around his own waist to tie again, leaving only a few feet of slack rope between them. He then tied the other end of the rope to the back of the sled. "Okay, all set, let's go," he shouted to her, and even in the dark of the storm, Carrie could see he was grinning.

"But—where are we going?" Carrie cried out, voice quivering. "Zack, level with me, please. Are we . . . ? Is this going to be it for us? Have we any chance at all to . . . to . . ." She couldn't squeeze any more words past the thick fear in her throat.

"Make it back home?" Zachary yelled over the noisy fury of the storm. "Of course we're going to make it, darling. Believe me, we're not in the slightest danger, we're perfectly fine." He leaned forward, pressing the side of his head against the side of hers. "We're not going far, just to cut some snow blocks to make us two shelters, one for the dogs, one for us. Now come on."

He turned away and began walking off, tugging on

the rope for her to follow. Every few steps he knelt down and tested the snow. After testing four times, he swung back, pulled on the rope to bring her up to him, and handed her the flashlight to hold.

"The trick of this," he yelled into her ear, "is to get snow frozen to just the right hardness. Once you do that, it's a shoo-in. Right here seems fine."

As Carrie held the light for him, Zachary began chopping into the snow with his short handled ax. In an amazingly short time he had hacked out a dozen blocks of snow, which together they arranged into a waist-high shelter, circular in shape with one narrow opening. After the first shelter was complete, they quickly constructed a second, the exertion keeping them both nicely warm. Together they pulled the sled over, Zachary led the dogs into the larger shelter, then he tossed the lap furs from the sled into the smaller shelter and motioned for Carrie to precede him in. After Carrie had stepped in, Zachary followed, drawing the sled into position tight up against the narrow opening. Spreading the furs on the frozen ground, he dropped down to his knees, then grabbed Carrie by the arms and pulled her down. A moment later he was lying in a curved position on the furs, with Carrie pressed down on top of him.

"There now," Zachary remarked happily, his arms holding her tightly against him. It was so quiet in their enclosure, with the noisy fury of the storm shut out by the wall of snowblocks, that she could hear him with ease. "The dogs are safe, we're safe. All safe and snug." Pulling her hood slightly back from her head, he whispered hoarsely into her ear, "And to keep ourselves warm, to stay alive, we'll make love."

"What?" Carrie squealed, instantly tensing, trying furiously to draw free. "Are you crazy? Aside from everything else, if we . . . if we take off our clothes we'll freeze to death!"

Zachary's arms around her tightened, forcing her down against him again. "I didn't mean we'd take off our clothes," he snapped impatiently. "Have you no imagination at all, for God's sake? Pretend I'm Mark, the man you're in love with, and I'll pretend you're Carrie, the woman I'm in love with, and we'll see if we can't get our blood to stirring, to race through our veins to keep us warm and safe. The Eskimos have known how to deal with storms for thousands of years, and to survive we'd better let their wisdom lead us. So relax and enjoy, for God's sake, woman!"

Carrie, feeling a bit subdued, tried to do as Zachary had said, letting go of her tension inch by inch, muscle by muscle, closing her eyes and feeling the comforting warmth of being so close to another human being. Zachary's arms around her held her close, her body lay on his, her cheek pressed his. For several moments she lay unmoving, just as Zachary did, then his lips pressed a quick kiss on her cheek.

"That's the way, sweetheart," he said. "Now let me teach you a little about nose rubbing, all right?" With a little chuckle he added, "This seems like a highly appropriate time. If I just place my nose against yours like this—" which he did as he spoke, "—and don't press hard or move my nose against yours, that simply means affection, nothing more. It says: I like you, I hope you like me. But if I press hard and start to rub, like this—" again he demonstrated as he spoke, "—that means something more, something far more than liking. It is meant to be, and for me is, highly erotic." After a minute or two more of rubbing his nose hard against hers, Zachary whispered hoarsely,

"How about you, Carrie? Does it do anything at all for you?"

"Yes, I—I like it too," she dared to admit, and Zachary immediately grinned broadly at her.

"In weather like this, it sure beats kissing," Zachary said. "When we're both this cold, if I tried to kiss you on the mouth, I could easily rip off skin when I drew away again, which is painful. So let's make out the way the Eskimos do." As Carrie reclosed her eyes, Zachary again moved his nose forcefully, erotically, against hers.

"You're a beautiful, extremely desirable woman," Zachary whispered into her ear a moment later. "I'd like to kiss you all over, from the soles of your feet to the top of your head. Just the slightest touch of you inflames me, sends passionate feelings storming through me." He shifted her body slightly then, to where she was half resting on the lap furs and he could move more freely. One of his hands came up to press against her cheek, then he moved it to her shoulder.

"Listen, sweetheart," he said then, pressing his cheek against hers as he spoke, "keep in mind that I'm wearing thick mittens, also that you're covered by very bulky clothing. Therefore if you don't get into the swing of it imaginatively, if you don't use your imagination for all you're worth, very little can be accomplished. Understood?"

Too caught up in feeling to trust her voice, Carrie merely nodded yes, she understood. Zachary drew a bit away, glancing down at her with a warm, loving smile.

"But, after all, lovemaking begins in the head anyway," he reminded her. "So take off the wraps and let your mind go. Get your pulse to pounding, your blood to racing, warm yourself up!" He leaned down then to press a quick little kiss on her cheek.

A moment later his hand left her shoulder and began caressing the base of her throat, then moved—inexorably, it seemed to Carrie—in the direction of her right breast, while Zachary, cheek pressed in against hers, whispered hoarsely to her that she had a lovely body, with lovely white breasts—how he'd wanted to kiss and caress her breasts from the first moment he'd laid eyes on her! In spite of the mittens he wore, the layers of warm clothing she wore, she could feel the pressure of his fingers, and her pulse raced wildly, blood pounding through her. She forgot to feel cold, felt almost too warm, overheated, almost unbearably excited. After a moment Zachary spoke softly into her ear.

"A man likes to be fondled and caressed too," he whispered. "Don't just be a zombie, sweetheart, love me back."

Somehow his words saying this sent even more passion sweeping through Carrie, and, her fingers trembling inside her thick mittens, she lifted her hand to touch Zachary's cheek first, then dropped her hand onto his shoulder, then began caressing his arm and chest as best she could through the bulky clothing he wore. This seemed to excite Zachary even more, to where his breath was quick and warm against her face, as hers no doubt was against his. Suddenly, as though forgetful of all caution, Zachary's mouth found hers, hotly, possessively, drawing up all of her being into the kiss. As he kissed her, his hands moved passionately down her body, while hers did the same, moving to caress him, and Carrie felt swept into feelings she had never experienced before, lost in the passionate heat of the moment.

As Zachary at last drew his mouth cautiously away from hers, Carrie felt a slight momentary discomfort but nothing more; then Zachary's mouth whispered into her ear, "Oh, baby, I love you so much, I want you so much!" and Carrie, beside herself, whispered back, "Oh, Zack, I love you too, I want you too!" Nothing mattered that moment but his closeness, his kisses, the wild storm raging through her. She had never before even imagined it was possible to feel this way. If this wasn't love . . .

Sometime later, after many more kisses, nose rubs and whispered declarations of mutual desire and love, Zachary rolled away, drawing her to lie again on top of him, and, her inner storm dying down, a great peacefulness rolling through her, Carrie cuddled warmly, comfortably against him and in time fell asleep, filled with a thoughtless exultation. Wasn't she safely close to the man she loved?

CHAPTER 6

In the morning the storm had abated. Though snow was still falling lightly and visibility was extremely limited, the wind had died down and the temperature had risen markedly. When Carrie woke, her eyes suddenly popped open, and she saw that it was daylight, also that she was alone in the little snowblock enclosure. As she pulled up to a sitting position, she glanced around and noticed Zachary approaching. A moment later he stood at the opening of the shelter, grinning down at her.

"Hi, sweetheart. If you're awake now, let's start back. I've got the team hitched up and ready to go."

Leaning forward, he took hold of her hands to pull her up. Once she was on her feet, he drew her close and kissed her, a warm and tender kiss that sent both excitement and an odd chill of fear racing through her. Did she dare put her fate into the hands of a man as ruthless and devious as Zachary was? Did he suppose that he had now destroyed the last of her defenses and from this moment on she was easy prey? Shivering with this thought, Carrie felt Zachary's arms tighten around her even more as he kissed her tenderly a second time.

The next moment, releasing her, he bent down and grabbed up the lap furs. Taking her hand he led her toward the sled. Though the wind had died down almost completely and was no longer a howling noisy fierceness in their ears, nevertheless snow was falling steadily, pelting against them, and Carrie, blinking, could see only a few feet in front of her face. Would Zachary be able to find their way back to the village now when the night before he had said they were completely lost?

Frowning, Carrie did her best to stumble along after Zachary as his hand pulled her along. Within a few seconds they had reached the sled. Zachary helped her down into the seat, then covered her with the lap furs. He crouched down alongside the sled, his dark eyes gleaming as he looked steadily and thoughtfully into her face.

"Are you all right, sweetheart?" he asked, his eyes searching hers.

"Yes, Zack, I'm fine," Carrie assured him nervously, quickly circling her eyes away, unable to meet his steady gaze. "But—do you know now where we are? Are you going to be able to find our way back?"

For a moment Zachary didn't answer. He stayed balanced on his haunches gazing thoughtfully at her. But after a moment, when she couldn't bring herself to face him again, he pushed up and answered, "Of course I will. I never travel up here without a compass. I've checked it out and have the sled headed in the right direction. Shouldn't take us more than fifteen or twenty minutes to reach Point Hope."

He took his position behind the sled, yelled out an

order to the lead dog, and the sled began moving smoothly forward. With senseless tears suddenly crowding into her eyes, Carrie slumped down lower in the seat and drew the lap furs up under her chin, memories of the previous night pouring through her. Over and over, as he'd held and caressed and kissed her, Zachary had told her he loved her, and at least three times she had responded that she loved him too. What had possessed her to tell him any such thing? But surely he realized that that had been said in the heat of the moment, inspired by the game they were playing to keep warm, to stay alive! Hadn't he told her to imagine that he was Mark, the man she loved? If he ever dared to make something of her declaration of love, she could always remind him coolly that she had simply followed orders and pretended he was Mark. That way . . .

So why am I crying, Carrie wondered, as more tears welled up and threatened to overflow. If in spite of herself she'd fallen for Zack. . . .

But that was nonsense! she snapped at herself, and within moments her tears had dried up. Zachary was simply an extremely attractive, physically magnetic male, and in her lonely, isolated position up here, separated from the one man she truly loved, it was perfectly natural and normal that she would find herself feeling physically drawn to him, aching for his nearness, his kisses, his embraces. But that kind of infatuation had little or nothing to do with love. To be caught in an Arctic storm, as she and Zack had been the night before, hopelessly lost, fearful for their lives . . . Her tears this morning were simply a delayed reaction, that was all, to the anxiety and terror she had managed to keep under control the night before.

But they'd been lost, supposedly, last night, while this morning Zack knew exactly which way to go to take them safely back to the village . . .

Pondering this, chewing on it, Carrie frowned and drew the lap furs up even higher, up over her mouth, covering her nose, to where only her eyes peered out. If Zack never traveled in this region without a compass, and the compass was in perfectly good working order this morning and could tell him the right direction to go, *just how lost had they really been last night?*

In what seemed no time at all Carrie could spot, through the light snowfall, the outlines of the village, and almost before she could sit up straight and prepare to dismount, the sled pulled up by the steps of the clinic and the lead dog stopped, panting and glancing around. Zachary stepped forward, offering a hand to help her out, and the next moment she was on her feet alongside the sled, safely home once again.

"Home again, safe and sound," Zachary murmured, smiling at her as he drew her close, then he pressed a warm and possessive kiss on her mouth. Held close against him, Carrie trembled but fought against it. Before long she managed to stiffen and draw free. She bit at her lip as she struggled to gain sufficient control to say what she felt compelled to say.

"How is it, Zack," she began at last, her voice thin and tense, with scorn trembling around the edges, "that you hadn't the least trouble guiding us back to the village by compass this morning when last night you claimed to be completely lost? Just how lost were we?" she demanded to know, gaining even more control over herself, anger pouring through her. "We were never lost, were we? You just claimed we were in order to—to force me to spend the night with you! Isn't that so? Please, for God's sake, for once don't lie!"

Zachary stood gazing steadily down at her, his gleaming dark eyes dancing outrageously. With a grin he said, "Easy now, sweetheart. That was a pretty fierce blizzard last night, you have to admit. I most certainly didn't make it up."

"Agreed," Carrie snapped icily, caught up in even greater fury. "I didn't accuse you of causing or inventing the blizzard, I simply no longer believe we were really lost in it, no matter what kind of storm it was. It didn't take us fifteen minutes to make it back here this morning, which means we could have made it home last night almost that fast, in less time than it took us to build those snowblock shelters. Admit it, Zack—we were never lost for a single moment, were we?"

Zachary laughed softly. Taking hold of her by the arms, he drew her close again, then whispered into her ear. "But now I've delivered you home again, perfectly safe and sound, so what is it you're complaining about?"

He tried to kiss her, but Carrie, in a mounting fury, tore herself free and backed quickly from him, staring at him with wildly enraged eyes.

"But—what about the fear, the cold, the misery I went through?" she exclaimed in outrage. "How dare you pull such a dirty, rotten trick!"

"What misery?" Zachary snapped, suddenly looking as angry as she felt. "My dear sweet Carrie, you didn't go through any terrible misery. The fact is you thoroughly enjoyed last night almost as much as I did. You even told me several times that you loved me, or have you forgotten that?"

The next moment he grabbed her, drew her close, and his full mouth came down on hers, so hard and possessively it was almost as though he wished above all else to hurt her, to force her to endure the misery she had complained of. In spite of herself, Carrie trembled. Her arms, as though of their own volition, crept up to wind tightly around his neck. As he held her and kissed her, with lessening fury and growing tenderness, Carrie could feel her whole body straining to get closer, ever closer to him. *Oh, Zack!* her heart cried.

Suddenly he ripped his mouth from hers, and whispered into her ear, "Now tell me again you love me, dammit, Carrie!"

"Oh, Zack, I can't!" Carrie drew slightly away.

Zachary pushed her instantly even farther away. "Then go to hell," he cried furiously. The next moment he swung away and strode off, disappearing into the light snowfall.

As Carrie stood staring after him, she became aware that tears once again stood thick in her eyes. How could she feel such lustful longing for a man toward whom she felt such deep distrust? Again last night he had proved how arrogantly ruthless he was, ready to go to any length to get those things that took his fancy. For some reason, possibly because her resistance made her a challenge he couldn't forgo, Zachary had decided that he must have her and he didn't care how he lied, cheated, tricked her, in his attempt to accomplish this. Oh, if only Mark were here so she could strengthen herself with his nearness, refresh herself in the great love they shared!

Carrie stood staring after Zachary long after he'd disappeared, then she turned, with a heavy heart, and mounted the steps into the clinic.

That afternoon the same Eskimo who had come to fetch her from the small hunting camp returned, bringing the sick man, who seemed much improved, with him. After a careful examination and further treatment, Carrie walked out with the two men and watched while they hitched the two sleds together, the one they had used to come to the village today and the one they had loaned to Zachary and her the day before, and then waved them off as they set out to return to their camp. After they'd left, Carrie, sighing, remounted the steps and returned inside.

That evening, feeling lonely and restless, she got out her box of letters and began rereading some of those she'd gotten from Mark. In one letter he had written:

"So you've met Zachary Curtis, have you? I've never had the pleasure (?) myself, but of course have heard of him. He's the kind of man you can't help hearing about. He's been in Alaska less than two years, knows nothing at all about our problems or our hopes, yet still he's got the almighty gall to pour in money and all the influence he can wield to try to force us to decide state issues his way, the arrogant rotter! We should take a page out of history, out of the old West, and tar and feather a carpet-bagging adventurer like that! I couldn't tell much from your letter, but I gather you didn't think too much of him on meeting him, as I'm sure I wouldn't either. I'm afraid were I ever to run across him I'd have a difficult time even being civil, that's how thoroughly I despise everything he stands for. Sometimes I get so angry just thinking about men like that I have difficulty letting go and relaxing, but I know I've got to learn to put irritations like that out of my mind and just take pride in knowing I'm doing the best job I can in the pursuit of those things I sincerely believe in, and to know that I have you with me, always loyal, in spirit right there in my corner fighting with me..."

After reading this, Carrie abruptly lowered the letter, then refolded it, and dropped it back into the box on top of all the others. She jumped up from where she'd been sitting on her bed, hurried to her closet, and decided to bundle up and go out for a walk. All day she'd been feeling restless, lonely, deeply upset, and she wasn't exactly sure why. A large part of it was anger, of course, a raging anger at Zachary for being the type of man he was, in particular for the lousy way he'd tricked her the night before.

Carrie drew on her parka, pulled the hood up into position, and hurriedly left her bedroom, then crossed through her treatment room. She passed rapidly through the tiny waiting room and stepped out onto the narrow wooden porch. After being shut up inside all day, what she most needed now was some fresh air and exercise.

As she strolled toward the village, Carrie told herself that what she desired above all else now was that Zachary would cease his pursuit of her and leave her in peace. After their hours together during the previous night, during which he had repeatedly vowed his love, to get so angry this morning and walk off that way—well, good riddance to him, she told herself.

If only she hadn't gotten so stupidly carried away as to tell him she loved him! Physical desire wasn't love—why couldn't Zachary see that? And surely physical desire was all he felt for her too, not warmly caring, enduring love!

In time Carrie turned reluctantly around again, walking slowly back to the clinic, and after undressing and climbing wearily into bed, she fell into a restless, dream-burdened sleep.

When she woke in the morning, Carrie told herself that Zachary would surely get over his anger and come back to see her that day. Once he did, she would insist on a reasonable discussion of their relationship, would make him see how impossible it was for them to continue seeing each other, and they would part again, forever, but in a friendly way, not with the angry frustration they both felt now. To part this way was a humiliating failure for both of them.

This was how Carrie reasoned it out, and every morning when she woke she told herself again that Zachary, over the worst of his anger, would surely return—before the brief winter day drew to a close, she would see him again.

On the sixth day following their night spent together in the storm, Carrie had an even stronger feeling than usual that this day would be it, Zachary would be back. Surely he'd had to leave the area once again on business this past week, but today he would return and come to see her. This is what Carrie told herself and before long believed. However, the brief daylight hours soon gave way to darkness with still no sign of him.

At about eight o'clock that evening, noticing flashing lights through the window of her bedroom, Carrie quickly pulled on warm clothing and hurried outside, lured by the fantastic display the night sky offered. As she had grown up in Alaska, she had frequently seen the northern lights, or aurora borealis. But she saw at first glance that the light show being splashed across the sky this night was one of the most spectacular she had ever seen. Watching in delight, caught up in awe at sight of the twisting, writhing contortions of colorful lights streaking across the sky, Carrie began striding quickly away from the clinic, leaving the village behind in her eagerness to get an even better, unobstructed view.

It was a clear, cold night, with no discernible wind, the snow underfoot frozen solid. Without stopping to realize in which direction she was going, Carrie began heading straight for the airstrip where planes flying into Point Hope landed.

As she hurried along, enchanted by the magnificent, darting streaks of light, Carrie heard a sound which she at first attributed to the fantastic auroral display in the heavens. Although she had long known that scientists tended to discount the notion that sounds accompanied the lights, she was also aware that almost all those living in the far north, those who were most familiar with the phenomenon, offered the same witness, that there *is* sound, a howling and whistling, accompanying the lights, and as she hurried along, she could very distinctly hear a sound, one which carried to her clearly through the cold, clear air.

Just as she decided, on the basis of her own senses, that the native peoples of the North were right and the scientists wrong, Carrie realized that what she was hearing wasn't the howling of the lights after all, rather a small plane was easing down to land on the airstrip. With an excited leap of her pulse, Carrie saw that the plane was the yellow-and-blue one that Zachary customarily flew.

I knew it! Carrie thought immediately, excitedly,

for all day she had felt that tonight would be it, Zachary would return. She stopped walking, leaving it up to Zachary to come to find her once he had dismounted from the plane.

Turning her eyes upward again, Carrie tried to recapture her earlier delight in the spectacular display, but she couldn't quite manage it; she felt too tense, too keyed up over what she assumed would be Zachary's imminent arrival at her side.

With her head back, her eyes fixed on the sky, Carrie felt herself drift tensely into a state of almost semi-shock, and although she fully expected someone to join her at any moment, nevertheless when a friendly voice greeted her, she was so startled she jumped.

"I frightened you," the voice said. "Sorry." To Carrie's deepening shock, it wasn't Zachary after all, but Matt Sanders, who stopped walking a few feet from her, and smiled rather shyly.

"Well—hello, Matt," Carrie said, her pulse, which had seemed becalmed, suddenly racing. But surely Matt was here with a message. Zack must be off somewhere on business, and was sending her word of this through Matt, as he'd done once before. Forcing out a friendly smile, Carrie added, "So how have you been?"

"Oh, fine." Matt motioned toward the sky. "Fantastic, isn't it? Naturally, being here in the Arctic, I've seen the lights quite often before, but this is one of the most dazzling displays I've ever seen. It almost makes one believe the old Eskimo legend that the lights are the spirits of the dead trying to communicate with the living."

"Yes, yes, it does," Carrie agreed as she turned her eyes up again to watch the sky.

Streaks of light, chasing and darting up and away,

appearing, disappearing, writhed across the upper sky. Then suddenly, for a moment, all lights faded away and the sky was dark, a terrible dead darkness; then again the bright red, yellow, blue, green, white, purple lights flashed on in pulsating waves and arcs, in gigantic undulating movements which swept across the whole heavens, then seemingly dived to the earth and melted away.

"You know," Matt said thoughtfully, "the scientists claim that the lights have never been measured closer to the earth than thirty-five miles, but when you watch them like this, that's awfully hard to believe, isn't it? I mean, just look over there. It's as though gigantic fingers of light were actually stabbing into the earth, isn't it? Or are my eyes deceiving me?"

"If they are," Carrie responded with a tense little smile, "then my eyes are deceiving me, too. I know what the scientists claim, yet watching you'd swear the lights actually swoop down and bathe the earth. It's hard to know what to believe, what you see with your own eyes or what you are told."

"Yes," Matt agreed, and they stood for a moment watching again in silence.

"I suppose you've heard what the various native peoples believe about these lights?" Matt asked her a moment later. "The most popular explanation is that the lights are the spirits of the dead playing ball with a walrus skull. Other tribes claim that the lights are the spirits of children whirling and twisting as they play and dance."

"And the whistling, crackling sounds," Carrie added quietly, "are the footsteps of the newly departed dead tramping around on the snows of heaven."

"Yes," Matt agreed, and grinned companionably at her, saying nothing more.

They watched the display for several more minutes, then Carrie turned away, murmuring that possibly it was time to return home. Matt fell into step beside her, and again Carrie tensed, wondering how soon Matt would deliver the message he had surely been sent to give her. How soon would Zachary be returning?

But Matt said nothing, simply walked along beside her, and before long they reached the clinic building.

"Well, Matt," Carrie said, "it was nice seeing you again and—" Her voice died away.

"Nice seeing you too," Matt responded, smiling. When Carrie didn't turn away or start up the steps, but rather stood silently, tensely gazing at him, he seemed to feel compelled to add something more.

"I flew in tonight," he explained, "to buy a few things from the village store. Niago was good enough to tell me I could always drop by in the evening and he'd open the store for me if I needed anything. Well, good-bye for now, Dr. Carrie. Zack will be pleased to hear I ran into you, I know."

"He—Zack—he's in the area now?" Carrie asked, distressed to hear anxiety creep into her voice.

"Oh, yes," Matt assured her. "We've been working about halfway up the coast toward Barrow, but in the evening we fly back to camp, Zack and the crew and I."

"And he—he's feeling all right these days?" Carrie couldn't keep from asking.

"Who, Zack? Oh, sure, he's feeling fine." Matt laughed. "The truth is that man has more energy than anyone I've ever known. After we've worked at top speed all day, I'm beat, but you know what Zack does? He and those crazy Eskimos, who never seem to tire either, every night this week they've been taking part in a tournament they set up, just for kicks, to work off some of their spare energy, I guess. They've rigged up this fancy obstacle course, and they take turns racing each other with snowmobiles. Well—I'd better be getting along now, I guess," Matt ended, and with another shy smile he turned and walked off.

Dazed, Carrie swung around and ascended the steps. Zack hadn't left the area. He'd been right here, in his nearby camp, this whole past week, and not once had he come to see her! Playing games with his men, racing around in a snowmobile, wasting time and energy mattered more to him than coming to see her! After his repeated declarations of love that night in the storm, after she had told him at least three times that she loved him too!

As Carrie entered the building, she felt consumed with rage. So much for Zachary's use of the word *love*, or his obscene *misuse* of it. Of course he loved her—as a spider loves the fly he plans to trap and kill, or a cat loves the butterfly he surreptitiously pounces upon and eats. So if he never comes back again, good riddance to him, Carrie told herself, crawling into bed with a sick and raging heart, repeatedly reassuring herself that she wasn't upset, rather she was glad to know that Zachary had now apparently lost all interest in her, which saved her from having to tell him to leave her alone. In the end it had all worked out.

Two days later—eight days after the night of the storm—Zachary came by the clinic to see Carrie again, arriving in the late afternoon just as her last patient was leaving. As she stepped into the waiting room and saw him there, looming so huge over the table where Irvana was sitting, Carrie felt her pulse leap with joy, then fury quickly rose in her and she began to feel cold, deathly cold, inside.

"Well—Zack," she said coolly, "did you want to see me about something?"

"Of course," Zachary answered, frowning, his dark eyes catching on hers. He had tossed back the hood of his parka and his thick curly black hair gleamed brightly, seeming to light up the tiny room. "But no hurry. If you're busy right now—"

"The woman who just left is the last patient scheduled," Carrie responded in the same cool voice. "I have a few notations to make on her chart, then I'll be right with you." Carrie smiled at Irvana, suggesting to her that it was all right for her to go home, then she turned and walked back into her treatment room.

After carefully closing the door after herself, Carrie walked the length of the room. Then she stopped, aware that she was trembling. So Zachary had returned, after all this time. Well, that was fine. She'd tell him calmly and coolly how she felt about him, about their impossible "friendship," and surely this time he'd take her words to heart and leave her alone. Let him go back to his wasteful snowmobile games, or find some other woman to confuse and upset. She wanted no more of him.

When she felt calm again, Carrie picked up her last patient's chart, made a few quick notations, filed it, and stood for a moment, breathing deeply. She had thought and rethought the words she wanted to say to Zack so many times it was as though they were engraved on her brain; all she had to do was throw the switch and they would surely pour smoothly out.

Before long and feeling completely in possession of herself, Carrie pulled open the intervening door and stepped back out into the tiny waiting room.

She saw at once that Irvana had left as expected,

and that Zachary was sitting on a chair in front of the table. Carrie stepped over to stand behind Irvana's table, letting her cool gray eyes move to Zachary's face.

"This is something of a surprise," she remarked. "You acted so angry the last time I saw you, going furiously off the way you did—"

"That wasn't acting," Zachary interrupted, rising slowly to his feet. "I *was* angry, sweetheart, so damn angry and disgusted I couldn't see straight."

"Don't call me sweetheart!" Carrie snapped, instinctively drawing her hands into fists and pressing them down on the table top.

"And why not?" Zack spat out mockingly, his gleaming eyes spitting fury at her. "I'm in love with you and—"

"And I want you to leave," Carrie cried, doing her best to drown him out. "Leave right now and don't ever come back! That's the only thing I want from you!"

Zachary's handsome face, scowling, flushed red. He stepped forward around the table, grabbed her by the arms, and pulled her toward him.

"Dammit, Carrie, that's utter rot!" he spat down at her. "No matter how hard you're fighting it, you're in love with me just as I am with you. If there's only one way I can prove it to you—" His mouth came smashing down on hers.

This kiss was the worst yet, seeming to draw her toward him from the soles of her feet up, draining her, pouring her being into him. As his mouth moved possessively, passionately, on hers, Zachary drew her ever closer against him, to where, even through their thick fur-lined clothing, she could feel his strength, his power and substance. After the first kiss, he drew back only for a moment, then he kissed her again and again. By then she had no will left, she had melted completely against him. Her body ached for greater closeness, every cell of her being cried out for joyful absorption into him.

As another kiss ended, Zachary swooped down and picked her up, lifting her as easily as though she were still a child. Carrying her, he strode into the treatment room. There he paused long enough to kiss her again, not only her mouth, but her cheeks, her closed eyelids, her throat, and Carrie had never felt such feverish waves run through her, firing her body from her toes to her fingertips, from the top of her head clear down deep into her heart. She could not fight him any longer, did not even want to fight; couldn't think, but did not want to. She let her clamoring nerves strain for and reach the joy they sought; for the moment she could resist no more.

After crossing the treatment room, Zachary pushed open the door to her bedroom and carried her quickly to her bed. Standing alongside the bed he kissed her again, a sweetly tender kiss that fired her even more, to where all through her she could hear her cells crying out their need for love, their need to possess and be possessed. Even if there was nothing left after Zachary finished with her, even if she had melted completely away into him, losing every part of herself . . .

"Oh, Zack!" she cried out passionately as his mouth moved away. "Oh, Zack!" and she could feel hot happy tears spring into her eyes as Zachary's mouth pressed once more, rather lightly, on hers.

Then suddenly, without warning, the mood was broken. In shock Carrie found herself being dumped unceremoniously down on the bed, bouncing on it from the thud of her fall. Her eyes flew open; she stared up into Zack's angry face. His gleaming dark eyes stared furiously down at her.

"I'm in love with you, Carrie," he spat out contemptuously, "and the day you finally wake up, the day you finally come to your senses and face that you've fallen in love with me too, that you want to marry me and spend the rest of your life with me, that's the day I'll make love to you, not before. So think about it—think about it good—you cold, unfeeling witch!"

With these words he turned and stalked rapidly out, leaving Carrie in a state of shock, staring numbly after him.

CHAPTER 7

It was holiday time with Christmas only a few days away. Carrie, having received word that Mark was flying home from the capital to spend Christmas week with his family in Anchorage, planned to close down the clinic for a week and fly to Anchorage, too, to see Mark and spend Christmas with him. It had been eight long months since she'd seen him, and in the last few months, especially since she'd gotten to know Zachary, Mark had tended to fade more and more from memory, to where she now had some difficulty in visualizing what he looked like, how his voice sounded when he talked—everything about him. This was more than a little disconcerting considering that she had known Mark for years. She met him during her last year of college, had been dating him steadily since, and had become engaged to him over three years before. In spite of this, she often had to remind herself these days that she knew him almost as well as she knew herself, and loved him totally. Once she saw him again . . .

Carrie packed a small suitcase and got ready to walk out to the small landing strip to catch her plane. She felt less tense and more at peace with herself than she had in weeks—in three weeks to be precise, ever since that dreadful night that Zachary had carried her into her bedroom and dumped her rudely down on her bed telling her arrogantly that he would not give her what she wanted, would not make love to her until she had agreed that she loved him and wanted to marry him.

Oh, the gall of that man, how he infuriated her! As though she wanted Zack to make love to her! Yet, in shame, she had to admit to herself that for a time there she *had* lost all will, that temporarily that night she *had* succumbed to the intense physical attraction she felt for him, and that had he gone ahead with seducing her, she wouldn't have stopped him.

Which just goes to show, Carrie told herself, folding two heavy sweaters into her case, what deep, extended loneliness can do to a person—make someone lose all reason and become a helpless victim of the senses. But thankfully Zachary had been decent enough, or arrogant or self-centered enough, not to take advantage of her momentary weakness that night, and never again, she vowed, would she slip into such stupidly uncontrolled behavior. Mark was the man she loved, the man she admired and respected, the one man on earth with whom she wished to share her life. Zachary Curtis was simply a recurring nightmare who had intruded into the lonely emptiness of her life here. But once she saw Mark again, once they'd had a chance to embrace, kiss, become reacquainted . . . Oh, how thrilled she was to be leaving here, if only for a few days, to be again with the man she loved!

Carrie closed her case, locked it and swung it up

from the bed. Since the night Zachary had carried her into this room she hadn't seen him once long enough to speak to him. The first few days after the incident she had felt so wrought up, so confused and angry, that she hadn't seemed able to think of anyone or anything but him. Awake or asleep she had ached to see him.

Though she hadn't had a chance to speak to Zack since that horrible night, she had on occasion caught a glimpse of him in the village, and each time, in spite of her strenuous efforts not to respond at all, her pulse had begun to race as excitement spilled through her. If only he would come to see her once more—but he didn't. Twice he had noticed her from a distance, and each time he had stared coolly at her, then offered her a slight arrogant nod before turning away, a nod which seemed to be a curt dismissal of her quite as much as it said hello.

Refusing to feel hurt over his new, cold attitude toward her, Carrie would tell herself immediately, while her cheeks burned hotly, that at last she had gotten her way and he was leaving her alone. Before long, if he continued to stay away, she would forget all about him, would once again be herself, calm and at peace.

Please, God, let it work out that way, Carrie thought, and kept her head high as she went about her business in the village and attended to her patients at the clinic. As soon as she had put in a one-year tour of duty at Point Hope, she would begin applying for other positions around the state, and once Mark had wound up his work in the nation's capital and could return permanently to his home here—well, everything was working out fine. All she had to do was exert a little more control to get her safely through the long lonely months that stretched ahead.

But for the moment there was an exciting break in her routine. Christmas was only two days away and she was closing down the clinic for a week to fly to Anchorage to spend the time with Mark and his parents. What a relief it was!

Carrie took up her suitcase and walked to the door of her bedroom, then swung half around to give the room one more quick glance. Suddenly a deep sigh rose in her. The day before she had run across Matt Sanders by chance, and he had mentioned that Zachary was out of the area right now, that he had flown to Anchorage.

This news had sent Carrie's pulse instantly to racing—Zachary was in Anchorage, as she would be within forty-eight hours!—but the next moment Matt added that he expected his employer back the following morning, and that the two of them planned to fly to Seattle, Washington, to spend Christmas Day there, with a sister of Zack's. So though Zachary had been in Anchorage, by the time she arrived there he would have left; besides, the chances of their running across each other in a city the size of Anchorage was minuscule anyway.

"Well—if I don't see you beforehand, have a lovely Christmas," she had said to Matt, smiling, and he responded by wishing her the same. She told herself that for her the holidays would indeed be joyful, for she had at last succeeded, apparently, in shucking off her unwanted suitor, Zachary.

Carrie walked through her treatment room, then through her tiny waiting room, her steps slowing more and more until in time she stopped moving at all. Matt had said that Zachary was due back at their nearby camp that morning. It was now approaching midday, and Zack might just possibly plan to drop by any minute now to wish her a happy holiday. She had told Matt that she was catching the Wein flight to Fairbanks that afternoon, and if Matt passed this information on to Zack . . .

Surely after all they'd been through together these past few months—the arguments, reconciliations, vows of love—surely he would drop by at least for a moment to say hello and wish her a Merry Christmas. Even people who couldn't stand each other tended to grow mellower and friendlier when the year-end holidays rolled around. The desire to smooth over differences and rid oneself of old resentments in order to start the New Year with a clean slate was almost universal, wasn't it? So—surely Zack would come.

Carrie put down her suitcase and suddenly spun around and walked back through the waiting room to the treatment room. She was a few minutes early for her flight and there was no point in rushing out to the airstrip to stand around in the cold wind waiting. The time could be put to far better use if she straightened up a few things in the clinic, brought the records of the last three patients she'd seen that morning up to date. As long as she watched the time . . .

Some time later, as she was rearranging a few things on the shelf of one cupboard, she heard the outer door to the clinic open, then a rapid stride start across the waiting room, and her pulse instantly began to race. If Zachary wanted to put old grievances behind them, if he would agree to keep things on a strictly "friends-only" basis from now on, if he gave her his word that he would never try physical persuasion again, and if, these things agreed on, he wished to offer her a friendly holiday hug and kiss . . .

With flushed cheeks and relieved, shining eyes, Carrie swung around, so sure that the person entering the room would be Zachary, that for a moment she felt almost dizzy with disappointment when she saw that it wasn't. Rather it was Leila, who was also flying out today for Christmas vacation and who wouldn't return until after the start of the new year. Carrie's disbelief that it wasn't Zachary was so strong that for a moment she felt completely disoriented, making it difficult to speak.

"Yes, Leila, what is it?" she managed to say after a moment, forcing out a smile. "Is it time to go, is that it?"

"Somewhat past time, I'd say," Leila boomed out goodnaturedly. "Or have you changed your mind about taking the flight out today?"

"Oh, no, no. I just—lost track of time, I guess. Thank you for coming for me."

Carrie crossed the room on legs that trembled slightly and headed out toward the waiting room, Leila following, shaking her head in teasing wonderment.

"Can't imagine how anyone could forget it was time to leave this godforsaken burg," Leila said and laughed. "For myself, I've been counting the days, the hours, even the minutes. For Pete's sake, let's go."

"Right," Carrie murmured, and with a troubled heart she left the clinic and started toward the airstrip, Leila chattering away at her side. Unless Zachary showed up at the airstrip to see her off, she would be flying off for Christmas without their having patched things up. Somehow, in spite of how estranged they had been these past three weeks, of how arrogantly he had nodded toward her the two times she had seen him at a distance in the village, in her heart she had still been sure that before the holidays, before she actually flew away to spend Christmas somewhere else, they would see each other, if only for a moment, and, letting bygones be bygones, they would at least smile and wish each other a warm and happy holiday season.

Zachary was not at the airstrip. The plane was ready to take off and had been delayed only by her tardiness in arriving, so Carrie had no choice but to hurriedly climb aboard, with an apologetic smile for having kept everyone waiting. Within minutes the small plane was in the air and Carrie, staring out her window watching the little village below grow smaller and smaller, did her best to fight down the distressful ache in her heart. Within hours she would be with Mark again, would be with the man she loved. Surely that was the only thing that really mattered. What possible difference did it make that Zachary had not cared enough about her even to drop by to say good-bye?

At the airport in Anchorage Carrie was surprised to see that not only Mark had come to meet her, so had his parents. She hurried to where the trio stood waiting for her, and with a happy smile she felt her fiance's arms go around her and his lips press a loving kiss on her cheek. The next moment Mark's mother, Norma, was giving her a hug, then Mark's father, Hugh. Carrie felt her heart swell with happiness, with the feeling of being home, back among the people she knew and loved. Though her own parents had moved to Anchorage when she was only five and she had grown up here, when her father had reached the age of sixty-five and retired from work, he and Carrie's mother had moved back to their home state, California.

"We can't take this cold anymore," her parents had explained. "Got to get back to where the hot sun can warm our bones." So Carrie had sadly seen them off, and a few months later had met Mark, and had begun steadily dating him. After Mark took her home to meet his parents and two younger sisters, it was as though his family became her family, and by now she had grown to love them almost as much as she loved her own parents. It was so good to see them again, to be home again if only for a few short days!

"Well, Carrie, girl, you're looking fine, just fine," Mark's father said, holding her at arm's length and looking her over. "Mother, doesn't Carrie look just fine?" he said, and Mark's mother, glancing around, immediately smiled and nodded in agreement.

The next moment they began walking along together, Mark's parents in front, Mark and Carrie a few feet behind. Carrie wound her arm through her fiancé's and gave his arm a happy, excited squeeze.

"Mark, it's so good to see you again," she exclaimed. "It's been so long."

Mark flashed her a quick little smile, then remarked, "Well, we've both been very busy, that's why it's been so long, but this year for me has certainly been a very stimulating and rewarding one and I'm sure it has been for you, too. Which isn't to say that we haven't missed each other," he added in the next breath, "for of course we have."

Carrie felt a first tiny wave of disappointment as she listened to these words. It wasn't that she disagreed with what he'd said, or felt in any way offended, but—had he always been this contained, so cool and composed, so . . . unemotional?

"I'm so very pleased your parents came with you to meet me," Carrie said next. "I'd almost forgotten how very much I love them, but, Mark, they're such won-

117

derful people. Which they'd have to be of course," she added, with a tiny teasing little smile, "to have produced a son as wonderful as you."

"Yes," Mark said, eyes dropping for a moment down to meet hers, his expression unchanging, as though he did not catch at all the spirit in which she'd tagged on that final comment. Rather than responding with a wide grin or a laugh or an equally ironic compliment of her, as she'd assumed he would or had hoped he would, his face had only taken on a slightly more smug look than it customarily wore, and his eyes—had they always had that closed, shallow look? Was this the man she had known and loved for so long?

With a sudden slight but uncontrollable shudder, Carrie held onto her fiancé's arm even more tightly, giving it another, prolonged squeeze, and as her eyes went forward she told herself she was simply tired, oversensitive. Naturally it would take a few minutes, at least, for her and Mark, after all their long months apart, to get used to one another again, to get back into sync. Just because he hadn't caught on to the fact she was teasing him a bit . . .

After they'd gathered up her one small case, they walked to the parking lot and climbed into the car, Mark's parents in front with his mother driving, Mark and herself in back. After they were comfortably settled, Carrie slipped over closer to Mark, her arm again wound through his, and she rested her head on his shoulder. Why didn't Mark kiss her? So far he hadn't, except for the one brief peck on her cheek when he'd first said hello, but now—surely his parents would understand, even if they happened to glance back and see. Not a long, hard, or passionate kiss, she didn't mean that—not the way Zachary, in forcing himself on her, customarily kissed her—just a warm, soft, I-love-you kiss on the mouth. Had Mark always been this distant with her, this undemonstrative?

Mark's mother backed the car expertly around, and pulled them into the traffic leaving the airport. For a moment Carrie closed her eyes, her head still resting on Mark's shoulder, but he seemed to be sitting so stiffly beside her, so tensely, she found it difficult to let go and relax. Within a very brief time she opened her eyes and pulled somewhat away, her gaze going again to his face, narrowing as she sat looking directly at him.

Apparently feeling her eyes Mark glanced around and smiled, then reached over with his free hand to give her hand on his arm a squeeze. "It's so good to be with you again," he murmured, with a loving little smile, and Carrie felt her heart immediately respond with answering affection. Mark did still love her, of course, as she loved him.

Mark's eyes turned forward again while Carrie continued to inspect his face. He was a relatively tall young man, though shorter than Zachary, with a slender, narrow build, fine dark hair a narrow, extraordinarily handsome face: light blue eyes under straight thin brows, a fine straight nose, a nice enough mouth, except—had his lips always been that thin? As he sat now, stiffly upright, staring straight ahead toward the front of the car, his lips were pressed together in a way that made them look very thin, and somehow unpleasantly stern and precise. Zachary's mouth, in contrast, had such soft full lips, and broke so easily into his wide boyish grin, while his gleaming, piercing dark eyes . . .

So just stop that right now! Carrie ordered herself. *Once and for all just forget that man!* Though she continued to hold onto Mark's arm, and his hand continued to press on hers, she dropped her eyes and felt a disconsolate wave of loneliness flow through her. It was going to take a little time after all, more time than she'd supposed, before she'd feel truly at home with Mark again.

After they'd arrived at Mark's parents' home, his mother served a late dinner, and as they all sat around the dining-room table under the sparkling glass chandelier Carrie remembered so well, she began to feel happy again, and at home. Neither of Mark's sisters was there; both had married within the last year and had moved into homes of their own, but aside from that it was like old times, eating dinner here with Mark's family in the pleasant, nicely furnished, fragrantly scented dining room.

As Carrie ate the delicious prime roast with all the trimmings, which had been waiting in the oven for their arrival home, she felt filled with memories, all of them happy and comforting. She had always liked Mark's home, not only because it was so quietly and tastefully furnished and Mark's mother kept it so beautifully, but also because, and this was an important part of her memories, it always smelled so nice, each and every room.

The dinner conversation had been light and bantering, and when they were finished eating the four of them went into the living room to sit, sip their after-dinner coffee, and settle down into more serious discussion of how things were going, especially for Mark in Washington in the course of the year. He had gotten home only a few hours before Carrie's arrival, so up to now had had little chance to brief his parents on how his lobbying efforts were going.

As Mark opened up and began to talk about his work, standing by the open fireplace and frequently assaulting the air with quick, rather hostile-looking jabs, Carrie found her thoughts wandering on occasion, which greatly disturbed her. Each time it happened, she sat up a bit straighter, refastened her eyes on her fiancé, and did her best to become absorbed in what he was saying, and to follow every nuance of his speech. That Mark's mother sat forward on her chair listening with total absorption, her eyes fastened steadily on her son's face, made Carrie feel even guiltier at her own lapses from strict attention. Mark's mother, like Mark himself, was a dedicated environmentalist, and had been active in numerous groups, including the Sierra Club, almost from the time Mark was born. It was only natural that she should now take such a passionate interest in how the Wilderness Areas Bill was faring in its highly disputed passage through Congress.

As Mark wound down his report, ending on a sourly pessimistic note, his mother jumped up from her chair and went hurriedly over toward him, reaching out a hand to touch his shoulder in support. Watching, Carrie felt the same flow of admiration for Norma Slaughter that she had felt since first meeting her. A woman of fifty, Norma was still remarkably attractive, tall, slender, energetic, a woman with clear sparkling eyes and a fine smooth complexion. But her lips, too, were very much on the thin side, Carrie noticed suddenly. They were thin, stern, rather self-righteous-looking in the way they pressed together. Could Norma really be the warm, loving person Carrie had always thought of her as being with those thin, prim, disapproving lips?

Her hand still gripping Mark's shoulder, Norma was saying, "Well, son, we knew from the start that it wouldn't be easy, that a measure of this kind—any environmentalist measure—is always up against the fiercest kind of opposition. Most people simply can't be forced to care about the future, about the rights of generations as yet unborn, all they care about is what they see as their own pressing needs of the moment, nothing else. But we knew we'd be up against that kind of shortsighted selfishness right from the start."

"You're right," Mark said. "As always, you're right." They stood for a moment in silence, mother and son, both with their thin lips self-righteously set.

"But," Carrie began suddenly, her pulse pounding with her own temerity, "why shouldn't the pressing needs of today carry some weight too? Why should only the future generations have rights? What about those living now?"

Zachary had argued this point with her one night, with casual good humor, his lips so soft and full. A shiver ran through Carrie as she thought of this—never pressing together self-righteously the way Mark's and his mother's were.

"What?" Mark exclaimed, his eyes darting to her, a look of outrage clamping down on his face. It was almost as though he wasn't so much upset by what she'd said as by the fact she'd dared to say anything, to offer an opinion he and his mother didn't share, possibly the very first time in all their years together she had ever done so.

For the first time since they'd come into the living room, Mark's father spoke. "What Carrie said," he repeated slowly, with great distinction, "was that the pressing needs of today should be given some consideration too, and that possibly those living right now have some rights too."

"I know what she said, father," Mark snapped rather petulantly, his eyes darting over to his father's face, then quickly away. "It was only that I couldn't believe my ears when I heard her say it. Up to now I've always thought Carrie had far too much sense to be taken in by the arguments of the common herd."

So anyone who disagrees is to be immediately put in place with an insult! Carrie began to feel a slight bit hot. Swinging around, she put her emptied coffee cup down on the end table, her fingers shaking just slightly as she did so, then she lifted her eyes to look directly over at Mark and his mother again.

"Is everyone who disagrees with you part of the 'common herd'?" Carrie asked, in the sweetest tone she could manage while her voice shook slightly. "For instance, I noticed some time ago that Governor Hammond, duly elected to the governorship by the voters of this state, has come out publicly against the Wilderness Areas Bill. Is he too dumb to know better too?"

Staring furiously across at her, Mark sniffed in answer, his cheeks flushing red. For an instant he acted as though that would be the only answer he'd design to give her, but then, after biting his lip, he spat out, "Well, what do you expect of a politician? Naturally he's got to go with the voters who put him where he is and who can just as easily kick him out. The fact that the governor is opposing the bill—" As though not knowing where to go with this statement, Mark cut off suddenly and offered an elaborate shrug, as though that explained everything, no need to express himself any further.

Leaning forward, getting ever more caught up into the argument, Carrie, trying not to let her voice exult too much, said, "Then you are willing to admit, Mark, that when Governor Hammond resists passage of the Wilderness Areas Bill he is to some extent at least reflecting the feelings of the people of this state? In other words, not everyone who opposes the bill is a vicious, greedy, Johnny-come-lately carpetbagger?" Carrie recalled how Mark had casually referred to Zachary Curtis in this fashion, as well as in even more damning terms in one of his letters.

Mark's eyes, which had swung away, came instantly back, hard, cold, blue eyes staring at her. Lips pressed tightly together, at first he simply stared, with a sneering expression across his face, but then he apparently couldn't resist throwing out, "Since when are you so enamored of what the common man thinks, the average voter, who for the most part doesn't know one damn thing about anything, all he cares about is dragging down his weekly paycheck and keeping his belly full."

Feeling suddenly victorious, and somewhat embarrassed and saddened by it, Carrie said softly, "But, Mark, doesn't the average voter have a right to feel concerned about those things, about working and earning enough to live on, to feed himself, his wife, and his children? Those living today *do* have some rights, or should anyway, and to keep our economy growing, not only here in Alaska, but throughout the United States, new energy sources simply have to be found, have to be drawn from the earth and put to use, or millions of people will be thrown out of work causing untold suffering. Zachary Curtis, whom I wrote you I met, mentioned to me one day—"

"I knew it!" Mark snapped triumphantly, his eyes gleaming with sudden new life. "You've been listening to that rotten worm, allowing that miserable, carpet-bagging, exploitive jerk to sell you a royal bill of goods! If all you can do now is mouth everything he said to you, without understanding a word you're saying—"

Jumping up, shaking with fury, Carrie cried hotly in answer, "Mark, dammit, just because Zack happened to mention—do you think I have no mind of my own at all, that I'm completely unable to think for myself? If that's what you think of me—"

Mark's eyes blazed across at her a moment longer, then he lowered his gaze, muttering, "All right, all right, I'm sorry. I didn't mean it quite that way."

"What other way could you possibly have meant it?" Carrie retorted, but her anger too had died down, and, feeling sick, she dropped back down on the sofa, quite as ready to end the fight as Mark seemed.

Mark's mother crossed the room quickly to sit beside Carrie, reaching over to take one of her hands, her face caught in an unhappy frown.

"Carrie, dear," Norma said, her voice quivering with earnestness, "no one's denying the validity of what you've said. Of course those living now *do* have rights, and there *is* this frightening problem of the energy shortage, and of what will happen to our entire economy if something isn't done, and done very, very rapidly. But, at the same time, dear—"

Norma paused, her shadowed, unhappy eyes fixed on Carrie's face. A moment later, after taking a deep breath, she went on, "But at the same time, dear Carrie, there is simply no avoiding the facts of what we have done—all of us have done—in exploiting and bleeding and destroying this earth we live on, the only earth we have. Once we've used it up, befouled it beyond any further use, there's no other place to go. If we continue the way we have been—well, I'm sure you know, my dear, that pollution of some streams and lakes, even oceans, has gotten so bad that if something isn't done, no one will be safe anymore, neither those of us living now nor any future generations, if there is any future for us the way we've been going. Water pollution, air pollution, land all too often callously ripped open, then left unusable, destroyed. It simply can't go on that way, my dear, it simply can't!"

Feeling deeply moved, Carrie moved her free hand to press it on Norma's two hands holding hers. "Norma, I know," she said softly. "I do know, and I have tremendous respect and admiration for the deep concern you've always shown, your willingness to devote endless time and energy, to work so hard for those things you believe in. At the same time, these issues, it seems to me, are now and possibly always will be extremely complex; there *are* two sides, or a dozen sides, to almost every issue—it's not quite as one sided, or as simple, as some people try to make believe it is." After saying this Carrie kept her eyes carefully fixed on Norma's face, making sure she did not glance even for a moment at Mark.

Norma gave Carrie's hands a hard squeeze, then pulled back her own two hands, sighing deeply. "Goodness knows, you're right. In fact, it's hard to see how anything could be more complex, less open to an easy and equitable solution. With this Wilderness Areas Bill, if we can possibly get it through Congress, we will be protecting vast areas of land for future generations, not allowing these beautiful areas to be exploited and destroyed. At the same time it has to mean hardship, and unfortunate dislocation, for innumerable native Alaskans, people who have lived on that land, hunted and fished there, for many thousands of years. It *is* a perplexing problem, Carrie, don't think I'm not very much aware of that."

"Thank you for telling me this," Carrie said, even more moved, feeling wonderfully close to Norma. "I've never heard you mention this side of it before, and when Zachary told me some of the things the bill would mean—"

"Would you get it through your head," Mark suddenly cut in in a shrill angry voice, "that mother and I have not the least interest in anything that lousy jerk has to say?"

Carrie's eyes swung around, her face flushing red at what had come as a totally unexpected attack. The last few minutes, talking so calmly and reasonably with Norma, she had all but forgotten that Mark was even there, had not kept it in mind that of course he was right there listening, overhearing every word. He could scarcely have made her feel more humiliated, more instantly put down, had he rushed over to slap her face.

Norma jumped to her feet, eyes blazing across at her son. "Mark, that's enough!" she cried, breathing hard. "In fact, it's more than enough. I think you owe Carrie an apology, a heartfelt one this time, and I suggest you give it to her right now. Otherwise I—I don't think I want you here in our home."

Oh, God, Carrie thought, feeling instantly sick again, sicker than she had felt at any time yet. As upset as she was at the way Mark had behaved all evening, not only at the things he had said, but even more at the smug, self-righteous expression she'd caught repeatedly on his face, the last thing she wanted to do was cause trouble between him and his parents. She was the outsider here, not Mark. This was *his* home, this the mother and father he had always loved dearly and who deeply loved him. That she should be the cause of such friction between them...

Carrie stood up, trembling in spite of herself, and glanced over toward Mark, not quite able to meet his gaze as she said, voice breaking, "Well, I'm truly sorry, Mark, that everything I've said tonight has seemed to offend you, and—and—"

As her voice quavered and died away, Carrie felt her hand being caught up and firmly clasped. "Carrie, stop," Norma said calmly. "You don't owe my son, or anyone else, an apology. Mark is the one who has been rude, closed-minded and thoroughly obnoxious all evening, and he'll apologize to you, as I said, or he can leave this house. I'm ashamed to think I have reared a son who could behave this way."

Mark's eyes, blazing out of his bright red face, glared across at his mother. He still stood in front of the open fireplace, tall, stiffly upright, his thin lips set, everything about him looking fiercely tense.

Mark's father slowly stood up, with a leisurely grace completely out of keeping with the extreme tension in the room. After walking over to stand by his son, he threw an arm around Mark's shoulders, saying in a warm, friendly voice, "Better do as your mother says, son. Come on, it's not that hard. You *have* been acting pretty badly, you know, and this is the girl you've loved for years and want to marry. What's so hard about saying you're sorry?"

Mark waited another moment, breathing hard, and then spat out, "All right, I'll do both, both apologize and leave this house. Carrie, I'm sorry," he said, and then he was stomping across the room, passing by where Carrie and his mother stood, striding hurriedly toward the front door. A moment later he had let himself out, closing the door hard behind himself, heading out into the cold Alaskan night, with Christmas only two days away.

Watching him leave, Carrie blinked hard against the hot stinging tears in her eyes she was determined not to let overflow.

CHAPTER 8

Carrie woke early the next morning and was instantly wide awake, remembering the incredible and dreadful happenings of the night before. For the first time in all the years they'd known each other, she and Mark had gotten into a bruising fight, one in which he had expressed scorn and contempt for her, and she had felt a matching scorn and total dislike for him.

After he'd gone stalking off into the freezing cold December night, no one in the house heard from him. For the first few moments after his angry departure, not a word had been said, then his mother, with a little choking sound, walked over to her husband and asked him please to go looking for Mark, who had gone off without even an overcoat, and had no car here and most certainly hadn't stopped to phone for a cab.

"He must just be stalking angrily off down the street," Norma said. "Go look for him, Hugh, please, and do your best to bring him back. I guess I shouldn't have said what I did, ordering him to leave that way, but—but his behavior was simply impossible, didn't you think so?"

Her husband patted her shoulder. "Stop blaming yourself. Mark acted like a stubborn jackass the entire evening and has only himself to blame. After all, he left of his own volition, you most certainly did not order him out. Maybe the night air will have cooled him off a bit by the time I catch up with him."

Hugh was crossing the living room as he finished his sentence. He opened up the closet by the front door, grabbed two overcoats, and put one on. He then put on a fur cap with earflaps and stuffed a second cap into a pocket of the spare coat he had over his arm. The next moment he went out through the door, closing it firmly behind him.

Norma stood by the fireplace again, staring unhappily over toward the door. Carrie, feeling suddenly tired, sank back again to the sofa. What a way for Mark and her to behave in front of his parents, as guests in his parents' home! And with Christmas only two days away!

Her cheeks flushing, Carrie said, "Norma, I wouldn't want you to think—well, that Mark and I fight like this all the time. The truth is we—we've never really had a big or serious fight before. I just don't know what got into us."

"I know, I know," Norma said quickly, brushing Carrie's explanation aside. With quick, tense steps she went over to the sofa and sank down beside Carrie.

"The truth is, Carrie," Norma said, her shadowed blue eyes on Carrie's face, "Mark seemed tense and strained from the moment he arrived today, which wasn't long before you flew in. I thought at first he was just terribly tired, but I'm sure now it was more than that. You two haven't—well, you haven't broken off your engagement or had a serious falling out, or anything like that, with the agreement that you'd put up a front until after Christmas for the sake of his father and me, have you, Carrie?"

"Not that I know of," Carrie said, doing her best to meet Norma's gaze directly, not to let her burning face betray a guilt she insisted to herself she didn't feel. "Certainly we haven't arrived at any agreement to break off our engagement, or to pretend that everything is still all right when it isn't. If anything's gone wrong," Carrie added, giving thought to this for the first time, "then it must have happened to Mark in Washington. Maybe he—well, maybe he's met someone else, and feels guilty about that. Maybe he wants to break off from me but just hasn't gotten up the nerve, or had the chance, to tell me yet. That would go a long way toward explaining what happened tonight, wouldn't it?" Carrie felt an odd, sick excitement jumping inside her as she voiced this thought.

"Yes, I suppose it would," Norma murmured, her cheeks flushing too as her eyes fell. A moment later she jumped up to say, "But for heaven's sake, let's not jump to conclusions, especially to wild, highly improbable conclusions like that. More likely he was just terribly tired, or maybe he was suffering from severe jet lag—flying such a distance can do that to one, you know—or—or maybe his digestion's acting up or he attended holiday parties before he left and drank a bit too much. Certainly he didn't act like himself, but that's the one and only thing we know at this point, so for now let's just leave it at that."

"Fine," Carrie murmured, leaning back on the sofa and for a moment closed her eyes. *Norma thinks that's what happened,* she thought in bewilderment, wondering how she would feel about it if it were true;

his own mother thinks he's met someone else and wants to break off from me. Somehow even the thought of it made her feel instantly empty and hollow. Mark had been such an important part of her life, such a pivotal part for so many years, it was hard to imagine adjusting to life without him, to a life she wouldn't be spending with him. Suddenly she thought of Zachary again, could again feel his warm full mouth pressing hard on hers, drawing every atom of her being to him through the kiss, and as a tiny shiver ran forcefully through her she sat up straighter again and opened her eyes.

"But as you say, Norma, no use jumping to conclusions," she said, forcing out a cool, weak smile. "I just hope Hugh catches up with him and brings him back, that's all. This is no weather to be out tramping around without even an overcoat, no matter how angry you are."

"Certainly we're all agreed on that," Norma said. "But for now I think I'll go fix us some coffee. I don't know about you, but I could use another cup, and surely Hugh and Mark will enjoy a hot cup the moment they return."

Rising, Carrie said, "May I help?" but Norma motioned no, that wasn't at all necessary, and walked hurriedly out of the room. Sinking down again on the sofa, Carrie sat staring absently at the open fireplace, her pulse pounding, as she wondered whether her speculation could possibly be true. Had Mark been on edge all evening due to his determination, not yet communicated to her, to break his engagement to her?

With a sigh, Carrie recalled the way he'd greeted her at the airport, with a stiff little hug and a quick, all but meaningless kiss on the cheek. Even in the backseat of the car, when he could have done better, he hadn't, he only pressed his hand rather coldly on hers, sitting stiffly upright on the seat, staring straight ahead. After their arrival at the house they'd been left alone for several minutes while Norma had gone to the kitchen, accompanied by her husband, to get dinner, and even then Mark hadn't really kissed her. Stepping up to her with a tense little smile, he had given her another very brief little hug, but no kiss, not even a quick peck on the check.

Well, it all added up, Carrie thought, her wide gray eyes staring unseeingly toward the fireplace grate. When Mark had first gone to Washington, he'd written her every day, then every other day, then once a week; this had soon been cut back to once every other week, and lately—well, this was the twenty-third of December and since Thanksgiving she'd gotten only one letter from him, a very brief one telling her of his plans to fly home for Christmas and inviting her to join him. No doubt just so he can tell me he has found someone else and no longer loves me, Carrie thought, and though her pulse skipped rather sickly at the prospect, it was more that she felt suddenly at loose ends, unanchored, than that she felt any great grief or heartbreak.

Better now than later, she told herself coolly, calmly; if I'm not the right one for him, if he's not the right one for me, better that we find it out before we get married than afterward. And she found it comforting to think that Mark hadn't been so cutting and nasty tonight just to be nasty; he'd been laboring under a terrible nervous strain, obviously. Even his mother concurred that he simply hadn't been himself. The fact that she could now see that he had undoubtedly had some excuse for his coldly rude behavior made her feel instantly, warmly forgiving of him. Once he'd gotten up his nerve to tell her the truth, admit to her what was bothering him—well, Mark, it's quite all right, Carrie thought, and with a rather contented little sigh she rested her head back, closing her eyes, hoping that any moment now the door would open and Mark and his father would come back in.

But this didn't happen, and time passed. Norma hurried back in, carrying a tray on which she had a silver coffeepot with four cups. Norma offered a cup to Carrie, who declined, then she nervously poured one for herself.

"I just can't imagine what's taking Hugh so long," she remarked anxiously. "How far could Mark have gotten, for heaven's sake? Oh, how I wish they'd get back!" Misty tears shone in her worried blue eyes.

Reaching over to touch the older woman's hand, Carrie said, "Now calm down, Norma. I'm sure everything's fine. By now Hugh has probably found Mark and they're standing outside, warmly dressed in their overcoats and caps, talking the whole thing out, father to son. I really don't think there's any cause for feeling worried."

Norma shot Carrie a glance that said how little she knew; there was ample cause to feel upset. After sipping her coffee a few moments, she jumped up, hurried to the front door to open it and stood in the doorway peering out. After several minutes, sighing, she reclosed the door.

"Well, so much for that theory, Carrie. They're most certainly not standing out there anywhere in sight. If only they'd get back!"

About ten minutes later the door opened and Hugh stepped back inside without Mark. "Sorry, honey, but I've been up and down the block several times. I even got the car out and went cruising slowly for several blocks each way, but there's simply no sign of him. But, for Pete's sake, honey, he's a grown man, he knows this neighborhood like he knows his own name, so there's certainly nothing to get all steamed up about. When he's cooled down enough to face how wrong he was, he'll come back of his own accord to apologize. Until then—well, hell, it's getting late, I vote we all go to bed."

As tired as she felt, it took Carrie quite some time to fall asleep, but when she did she slept soundly and well. When she woke in the morning and remembered what had occurred, she lay in bed staring up at the ceiling, wondering where Mark was now, where he had spent the night, whether he would phone the house today or, possibly, just walk back in. But surely, when tomorrow was Christmas, tonight Christmas Eve . . . With a sigh she climbed out of bed and drew on her robe.

An hour later everyone in the household was up, and they sat down at the dining-room table for a nourishing breakfast that Norma had nervously prepared for them: bacon, eggs, toast, orange juice, and coffee. Very little was said; no one made any mention of Mark. When the phone rang just as they were finishing their coffee, Norma jumped up like a shot and ran to answer it.

Within a few minutes she was back, relief shining in her clear blue eyes. She stepped up behind Carrie, put her hands to Carrie's shoulders, then leaned down toward her to say softly, "It's Mark, dear, and he wants to know whether you'd be kind enough to go to the phone to talk with him. He says he phoned for a cab last night from a house down the block, neighbors we've known for a long time, and spent the night comfortably in a hotel downtown." Norma straightened up, circled the table back to her chair, and sitting back down she poured herself another cup of coffee, her face looking deeply relaxed and happy.

Jumping up, nodding that of course she'd take the call, Carrie brushed her lips hastily with her napkin and hurried out to the phone, her pulse skipping lightly. Would Mark tell her now, over the phone, or —well, more probably he'd ask for a chance to talk to her in person. "Yes, Mark?" she said, in a warmly friendly voice after she'd picked up the receiver.

"Carrie? Carrie, thank you so much for agreeing to talk to me. First I just want to say that I'm most certainly not proud of the way I behaved last night, the fact is I'm pretty damned ashamed of myself. Secondly, Carrie, if I came to the house would you give me a few minutes' time to talk to you, to explain why I acted as I did? The truth is I was feeling very upset and I'd like to tell you why. Would that be all right?"

Carrie responded quietly, with deep sincerity, "Of course, Mark, please do come over and let's talk this out. I think that right now that's the most important thing we could possibly do, hopefully to clear the air and get everything straightened out. And, Mark— please, Mark—for your parents' sake if not for your own, please come planning to stay. After all, tomorrow's Christmas. No matter what the problem is, for your parents' sake let's put up a united front and all of us have a friendly holiday, all right?"

"Suits me," Mark said. "And, Carrie, thanks again. I'll see you in about half an hour."

"Fine," Carrie said, and with murmured good-byes, they both hung up.

In about thirty-five minutes Mark arrived, stepping in through the front door with flushed cheeks and shadowed eyes. His mother rushed to give him a welcoming hug, then discreetly retired to the back of the house where her husband was, leaving Carrie and Mark alone. In an embarrassed silence, Carrie's pulse tripping nervously, they walked into the living room together and sat down a few feet apart on the sofa. Then Carrie raised her cool gray eyes to meet the gaze of her fiancé, her pulse slowly calming down again.

"All right, Mark," she said softly. "Please open up and tell me what the problem is, no matter how—how worrisome it might seem to you. Surely honesty is the one thing I do deserve."

"Right," Mark agreed, nodding, his shadowed, tired-looking eyes meeting hers. He opened his mouth as though to begin, then reclosed it, biting at his lip. Carrie reached over to place her hand on his arm in encouragement, so sure of what he planned to say that when he finally began to speak, she could hardly believe what he actually said.

"All these months I've been gone," Mark said, his eyes dropping to stare down at the floor, his cheeks losing their flush and growing pale, "on the one hand I've been terribly busy, and on the other—well, I couldn't seem to help myself, right under the surface of my mind I began to get more and more worried, and no matter how hard I tried to tell myself I was worrying needlessly, nevertheless the worry persisted."

At this point Mark's eyes came up, looking even more strained. His narrow, handsome face caught in an anxious frown, he went on, "I mean, Carrie, at first you wrote me almost every day, then before I knew it the letters came only every other day, then once a week, then even less frequently, to where it seemed to me I practically never heard from you. Of course I knew you were very busy, I kept reminding myself of this, but—well, underneath, deep inside, I began to panic, I guess, though I don't think I ever faced that I had. Then yesterday, when we picked you up at the airport—"

Mark paused a moment, brushing a hand against his nose, his eyes wandering away again. With a voice that sounded somewhat choked, he continued, "When I first caught sight of you, walking toward us, Carrie, I felt such joy, such love, I couldn't wait for you to reach us so I could grab you and kiss you, but then when—when I put my arms around you, wanting to kiss you, the way you sort of turned your face away, as though to tell me I was not to kiss you, even to say hello—"

"I did not!" Carrie exclaimed, drawing a bit away, shocked to hear Mark make such an accusation. "Surely I didn't!"

Mark's eyes moved around to meet hers, a crooked smile pulling on his mouth. He shrugged. "Well, maybe you didn't, I don't know, but I thought you did. It seemed to me that the moment I put my arms around you, you stiffened, that you felt so uncomfortable you couldn't wait to draw free again."

His smile broadened, a pained smile that twisted across his mouth. "And that's all it took, suddenly all the fears I'd been sitting on so tightly for all those months exploded through me and I went a little crazy I guess. All I could think of as we were leaving the airport, climbing into the car, driving home—well, that's all I could think about, that you no longer cared about me, that you'd drawn so far away I'd never get you back. And I kept remembering your letters, the few you ever bothered to write me, and how in every letter you wrote me about that man, Zachary Curtis, wrote about him on every page of every damn letter you wrote."

"Oh, no!" Carrie cried softly, one hand going to her mouth, her suddenly fear-filled eyes catching on his. "Surely I didn't do that?"

By then a little color was returning to Mark's face; his eyes looked a bit less anxious. He laughed briefly, shrugging again. "Well, it seemed to me you did. That time he rescued your pregnant patient—I kept telling myself that of course that was an important and dramatic happening in your life, in anyone's life, and I shouldn't make too much of it, but you went on and on about it for four pages, making him sound like the most heroic male who had ever walked the earth, and the plain truth is I was eaten up with jealousy, I guess. Add to that how lonely I felt, and how far away you seemed to have slipped—"

Again Mark paused, then he turned to face Carrie directly, his eyes fastening on her face. With a little shrug he said, "And all of this had me so upset that last night, when we got into that argument—" His voice died away, then after a deep sigh he said, "I was so happy to see you again, but felt you had no feeling at all about seeing me, and I just couldn't take it, so the first slight excuse I had, I lost all control and blew up, that's all. I'm not saying there's any excuse, I just wanted you to know what had caused it, all right?"

"Oh, Mark," Carrie said, tears flooding into her eyes, her voice quavering, "I had so looked forward to seeing you, too, and I—I couldn't understand why you didn't even kiss me."

The next moment she was in his arms, and Mark's mouth came down warmly on hers. As Mark held and kissed her, Carrie felt suddenly frightened, suddenly empty and sick. Mark's kiss—why couldn't he kiss her more ardently than this, injecting more excitement, more passionate possessiveness into the way his lips met hers? So much of her felt untouched, unmoved, coolly aloof.

Oh, Mark, you'll have to do better than this, far better than this, Carrie thought in distress, then immediately sat on the thought, telling herself she was delighted that they had now straightened out the problem between them, that from this moment on everything would be right again, warmly loving and close. After all, this was Mark, the man she'd known for so long, the man she respected and admired as well as loved. Surely from this moment on everything would be fine.

Later that day Mark's parents seemed deeply relieved and happy to see that their son and his fiancée had smoothed over their quarrel, and dinner that evening was a friendly, festive occasion. Christmas Eve passed very pleasantly, with the exchange of gifts, then Hugh played carols on his organ. At a little after midnight everyone said good-night and retired, Mark drawing Carrie close for a quick good-night kiss at the door of her bedroom.

Christmas Day passed just as pleasantly, and the day after that, by which time Carrie had all but forgotten how upset she had felt, first at the falling out she and Mark had had, then at their reconciliation. By then she had slipped back into the comfortable rut she and Mark had long since carved out for themselves, in which they jogged along together smoothly, with little friction, each always friendly and carefully polite with the other, and Carrie found it increasingly easy and non-threatening to have it that way. By then she was reaccustomed to the lack of excitement in Mark's kisses, to the fact that his nearness neither frightened nor upset her; and this too began to seem natural and the way love should be, easy and comfortable.

And then three days after Christmas, about two in the afternoon, a dreadful thing happened: she and Mark ran across Zachary Curtis! Mark had told her that he wanted to go down to the federal building to see an official in the Department of Interior, and he'd asked her to accompany him. Having nothing better to do and pleased to be getting out of the house for a time, Carrie agreed. It had never crossed her mind that they would run across anyone she knew, let alone Zachary, whom she assumed had left Anchorage days before.

Carrie and Mark had been walking down a corridor of the federal building when a door about fifty feet ahead of them opened and a man stepped out. Instantly recognizing the man as Zachary, Carrie felt her pulse bang, her throat go dry. Why was Zack still in Anchorage, she wondered wildly; Matt had told her that Zack was leaving Anchorage before Christmas. But there was no doubt it was he, and she felt immediately so upset, so wrought up, her step faltered and her knees went weak. Mark reached out to touch her arm.

"Honey, what's the matter?" he asked curiously. "Your face is as white as though you just saw a ghost."

"No, not a ghost," Carrie managed to murmur over the huge nervous chunk in her throat. "But that man up there, in the dark green suit, that—that's Zachary Curtis," she ended in a hoarse whisper, scarcely able to draw in breath.

"It is?" Mark said in surprise, his eyes racing forward. "Well, for Pete's sake, sweetheart, that's no reason to look so scared. I realized days ago how stupid I was to feel jealous." Mark's hand grabbed for hers. "Come on, let's walk up there and you can introduce me. I'd very much like to meet him."

"But—but why?" Carrie stuttered, her legs feeling

even shakier. Just the sight of Zachary here in the city where she had never expected to see him filled her with distress. One glance at him and it was as though she could again feel his arms pulling her close, his mouth passionately possessing hers. *Oh, I don't need this, I don't!* Carrie thought in immediate despair, furiously batting back nervous tears that had sprung to her eyes; this is the very last thing I need!

But Mark, intent on his own wishes, seemed not to notice how upset she felt. Holding her hand he pulled her forward, a slight tense smile parting his mouth. Within seconds he had drawn her up to within a few yards of Zachary, and Zack, hearing someone approach, glanced up and saw them. His face lighting up, he stepped quickly forward to meet them.

"Carrie, what a delightful surprise!" Zachary thrust out his hand to her, his gleaming dark eyes seeming to envelop her, to devour her. Doing her best not to tremble, Carrie put out her hand, allowing it to be swallowed up in Zachary's large, warm one.

"And this must be the young man you've told me about, your fiancé." Zachary's dark eyes switched from her to gaze steadily at Mark; he let go of her hand to shake hands with Mark. "Hi, I'm Zachary Curtis."

"Mark Slaughter," Mark murmured, his pale face flushed.

"I suppose Carrie told you she and I met up in Point Hope," Zachary said, still grinning. "When we learned of the clinic she'd opened there, we even moved our base camp to be closer to where she was. It's comforting to have modern medical attention so close at hand."

As he said this, Zachary's piercing dark eyes moved to fasten again on Carrie's face with such force it seemed to Carrie she might easily be drawn into them, sucked into the whirlpool of his warm, gleaming eyes, wherein she would surely drown. She drew herself up even more stiffly, biting nervously at her lip as she looked at him, seemingly unable to move her gaze away.

"But—but I thought you'd left Anchorage days ago," she managed to stutter out, her cheeks by this time burning up. "At least Matt told me you were expected back there at camp the morning I left."

Memory of that morning, of the way she had stalled anxious minute after anxious minute, hoping against hope that Zachary would turn up to say good-bye and wish her a happy holiday, swept up through Carrie, making her feel even less in control, more exposed and vulnerable. From the first day she'd met this man he'd been able to cause such chaotic misery within her that a loving God would surely release her soon from such unrelieved torture. With Mark at her side, protected by her calm and peaceful love for him, with effort she should be able to reach proper balance even without God's help. Thinking this, Carrie found the courage to face Zachary, to do her best to feign polite interest as he answered.

"You're right, I had hoped to be gone from here several days ago," Zachary said, still grinning. "But you know how it is when you get tangled up with the government. Even with the current situation, an energy crisis so severe that it threatens to bring all of the western world grinding to a wrenching halt, everything barely crawls. There are certain government bureaucrats who I swear would continue to go by the book, all wrapped up with miles and miles of pretty red tape, even on Judgment Day." Zachary laughed briefly, then ended, "Which is why I'm still here, instead of exploring for much needed gas reserves up on the Arctic slopes." His eyes, which had moved to Mark as he spoke, moved back to Carrie's face again, warm gleaming pools which threatened to draw Carrie in.

After nervously clearing her throat Carrie remarked, "Then—then you weren't able to get away for Christmas at all? I'm sorry to hear that. Matt told me you planned to fly down to Seattle to spend the day with your sister."

"Oh, we did that, all right," Zachary assured her, in a voice that was somehow softer, less compelling, as though he were mindful of the distress she was in and wanted to help her through it. His grin dying away, he added, "Matt came here to join me and we flew down to spend two days in Seattle, but now it's back to the same old battle, trying to cut through some of this endless red tape. But how soon will you be heading back?" he asked Carrie quietly, in a concerned and thoughtful voice.

"Oh, in a day or two, before New Year's," Carrie answered quickly, plunged into an even greater agony of nervousness by Zachary's obvious concern for her. Even more than usual, she felt almost unendurably threatened by Zachary's nearness. Once again she was assailed by the familiar, irrational fear that his physical magnetism would draw her irresistibly toward him, and into him, to where she would melt away and cease to exist. She knew how insane such panic was, yet still she felt it, could not seem to fight it down, and in extreme agitation she turned to Mark, her gray eyes beseeching.

"Well, Mark, we—we'd really better be getting along now, hadn't we? Nice—nice to see you again," she added to Zachary, eyes down, her voice little more than a ragged whisper.

Mark took Carrie's arm and as she stepped away

past Zachary, she felt the pressure of her terror let up, began to feel safe and whole once more, only to have this shattered completely a moment later as Mark swung back, and with a smile on his face that Carrie's eyes, darting up, noticed at once, Mark said to Zack: "Well, maybe we'll see you around again sometime. I really enjoyed meeting you."

"And I you." With a sudden new grin, Zachary went on, "Say, I've got an idea. Why don't we meet tonight for dinner, or tomorrow night? I'll bring along a friend and the four of us would have a chance to talk more fully and get acquainted. Would you be able to?"

In immediate shock Carrie opened her mouth to protest, to insist that such an engagement was out of the question, she and Mark were busy and couldn't possibly make it. But before she could get her tongue untangled enough to speak, Mark thrust out his hand to Zachary, smiling broadly.

"Why, thank you, Mr. Curtis, that sounds great. Why don't we make it for tonight? I'll make reservations for Don Chinn's Club Chinatown, if that's all right. Shall we say around eight?"

"Perfect," Zachary said, bursting forth with a complacent little laugh as he and Mark shook hands on the date.

The next moment, his hand holding her arm, Mark began leading Carrie off down the corridor while Carrie tried frantically to deal with her shock.

"But—but, Mark, for heaven's sake, why did you agree to that?" she hissed frantically the moment she felt they were out of earshot. "I know what you think of that man—in your letters you were certainly explicit enough—why did you ever accept his invitation?"

Carrie stopped walking, her legs too weak to carry

her any farther. Turning toward Mark, she faced him with frightened, beseeching eyes, trying to make him see what an impossible situation he had put them in. There was no way she could endure spending an entire evening with both Mark and Zachary!

Mark laughed softly, a look of cold cunning in his pale blue eyes. "Honey, I didn't say I liked the man, did I? I simply said I'd enjoyed meeting him, which I had. And as for having dinner with him tonight, I was tickled to have the chance. Remember the other night when you were bringing up various points against the Wilderness Areas Bill? Sweetheart, those arguments weren't new to me, I've heard every one of them before, but still I figure it doesn't hurt to get to know everything you can about the strength of your enemy's position. From what I hear, Curtis is pouring plenty of money into the Citizens for Management of Alaska Lands, the group set up to oppose our bill, and the more I can learn about what motivates him, what his basic concerns really are, the better position I'll be in to fend off his blows and bring him, and all others like him, to their knees. Can't you see that?"

"But—but—" Carrie stuttered, hot tears now stinging her eyes.

"But nothing," Mark quietly overrode her, grabbing her by the arm and walking forward with her again. "I don't mean I'll get into an open argument with him, or make myself obnoxious the way I did the other night with you. if that's what you're afraid of. I give you my word I'll behave myself, but at the same time I wouldn't miss this for the world. How often does one get the chance to break bread with an avowed opponent, so you can measure him up close and see if you can't spot his Achilles heel? Or determine whether he doesn't have a soft underbelly where you can attack him with the most success. I'm sorry that you seem upset, but, sweetheart, this is the kind of thing you'll have to grow accustomed to once we're married. Political maneuvering is a complex, many-faceted operation, but, Carrie, it's exciting too," Mark concluded, giving her arm a little squeeze, "and once you get into the swing of it, I'm sure you'll enjoy it as much as I do. In any case, we've already made this dinner date for tonight and we're most certainly going to keep it."

We didn't make this date, Carrie thought in righteous anger trying to fight down her fears, *you* did, and without so much as even glancing my way, much less asking whether or not I wanted to go. But it was all too apparent, as she peeked around once again at Mark's flushed, excited face, that it would mean an open, pitched battle if she refused to honor the dinner invitation he'd just accepted from Zachary, so she supposed there was nothing to do but to repress her resentment, conquer her nervous anxiety, and go through with it.

But—could she survive an evening spent in the enforced company of those two men, the man she respected, loved and hoped to marry, and the man with whom she was so physically taken that if he but touched her arm he was apt to shatter her?

CHAPTER 9

They arrived at the Club Chinatown at about fifteen after eight that evening, and were told, on inquiring, that yes, Zachary Curtis and his companion had already arrived. As a waiter led them to a table, Carrie saw in shock that Zachary's friend was not Matt Sanders, as she'd taken it for granted it would be, but a stunning young woman.

In immediate panic Carrie asked herself why she had failed to realize that naturally Zack had meant he'd have a woman friend with him. Somehow his pursuit of her back in Point Hope had seemed so arrogant and ruthless, his desire for her so compelling and lustful, it had been some time since she had allowed it to cross her mind that he might know other women and pursue them with the same zeal. But of course a man like that would chase after new women wherever he happened to find himself. Hadn't she known from the first that that was the kind of cheap, exploitive male he was?

Walking behind the waiter with Mark a step behind

her, Carrie thrust her chin up a little higher and told herself that the fact Zachary was there with a woman companion would simply make the evening easier on her. Had she been the only woman with three men, political issues might have been raised and the ensuing argument quite possibly could have gotten completely out of hand. The way things were, with a lovely young woman friend there to keep Zachary's mind off business, the chances that this would happen were greatly diminished. Consequently, Carrie told herself, catching her breath and fighting down her shock as best she could, she felt very grateful. Besides, having a young woman with him would certainly keep Zachary from making any awkward moves in her direction in front of Mark, and also would surely keep him silent about certain things that had happened in Point Hope. At least she most fervently hoped so.

As they arrived at the table and Zachary, grinning, rose to his feet to welcome them, Carrie blurted out, not able to stop herself, "But where's Matt? I assumed that he would be with you tonight."

Zachary's grin died away as surprise flashed through his gleaming dark eyes. "Carrie, I'm sorry, it certainly wasn't my intention to mislead you. I'd have asked Matt along but unfortunately he had other plans." Zack's eyes dropped to his young woman companion seated at the table. "Linda, this is the very dear friend I told you about, Dr. Carrie Addison, from Point Hope, and Carrie's fiancé, Mr. Mark Slaughter. Carrie, Mark, a dear friend of mine, Linda Grant."

"How do you do," Carrie murmured to Linda, feeling distressed at the warmth that was already pouring into her cheeks. She caught the quick smile with which

Mark greeted Linda, then took her chair at the table as Mark helped her into it. She sat across from Linda, with Mark at her right hand, Zachary at her left. The palms of her hands felt damp and clammy, her fingers trembled, nervous tremors kept running down her arms. If she didn't get better control of herself than this, she'd never get through this dreadful, dreadful evening!

"How lovely you look tonight, Carrie," Zachary addressed her in a soft caring tone, in a tone an adult might use to a child he was trying to soothe and comfort. With an immediate spurt of anger, Carrie lifted her wide-set gray eyes and managed to look directly over at Zack, eyes spitting fire. He needn't think he had to patronize her that way, or that she wasn't able to hold her own under these circumstances or any other! Just because she felt a slight bit nervous . . .

"Yes, doesn't she?" Mark agreed, smiling at Carrie. Yet the smile wasn't reflected in his pale blue eyes, which, it seemed to Carrie, had the same coolly calculating look in them she'd noticed that afternoon just after he'd made this engagement for tonight. That look made him seem almost a stranger to her, one she wasn't sure she liked very much.

"But certainly not one bit lovelier than Linda," Mark added without a break, his eyes switching over to settle on Zachary's "dear friend." "I have to give you credit, Mr. Curtis, as the evidence would seem to suggest you have excellent taste."

"Considering that that remark was offered by a man whose own taste is clearly flawless, I thank you, Mr. Slaughter," Zachary responded good humoredly, grinning. "Now will you and Carrie have something to drink?"

"Call me Mark, please."

"My pleasure. And I'm Zachary. Now what will you have?"

As this exchange was going on, Carrie found herself able at last to glance directly across the table at Linda Grant. Her heart sank as she realized that her immediate reaction, some minutes before, that the woman with Zachary was a stunner proved only too true on closer inspection. Linda, who sat erectly on her chair with a little smile playing around her mouth, had long, gleaming dark hair, a lovely high forehead, thin brown brows over light brown eyes, a finely sculptured nose, and nicely molded lips which broke over perfect, even white teeth. Her complexion was light and smooth, her expression pleasant and friendly. As she caught Carrie's eyes surreptitiously inspecting her, she smiled even more broadly, warmly, and leaned a little forward to speak.

"It must be truly exciting to have such an important job, to do something so different as to run a clinic up in the Arctic for the Eskimos," Linda said, sounding as though she sincerely meant what she was saying. "When Zack told me about you this evening, and that you and your fiancé were going to join us for dinner tonight, I can't tell you how pleased I was."

"Well—thank you, Linda," Carrie murmured, her heart sinking even lower. Linda was not only lovely to look at, and beautifully dressed in an off-the-shoulder dark blue evening gown, she also seemed to be a very warm, genuine human being, quite possibly a woman who could not only inspire desire in a man like Zachary but could also capture his respect and his heart. Carrie thought about asking Linda whether she was employed, and if so at what, but she'd never found it easy to reach out to others, even in conversation, and she couldn't seem to do so now.

Instead of speaking she let her eyes drop, and nervously intertwined her fingers in her lap. The reason she and Mark had been a little late in arriving was that she'd spent two frantic hours trying to decide what to wear, wishing hopelessly that she'd had time to shop for a new dress. But she hadn't; she'd had no choice but to make do with something she already owned.

After she'd finally, unhappily, made her choice and finished dressing, she'd caught the look of surprise in Mark's eyes when he'd seen what she was wearing, the same old gray dress he'd seen her in so many, many times before.

Heart full of dismay, she'd said, "You don't think I should wear this, Mark? You always used to say it was your very favorite."

"Of course, and it still is," Mark had said quickly, covering up. "You look fine, perfectly fine." He called good-night to his parents and led her out of the house.

So here she sat, in a six-year-old dress, feeling pale and colorless and decidedly unattractive pitted against the radiantly charming young woman seated across the small table from her. On top of that, Carrie had to admit in sick dismay, that not only was Linda Grant a far more beautiful woman than she was, she was also, to make matters infinitely worse, a much warmer, friendlier, more outgoing person. What was that awful thing that Zachary had said about her so many, many months before, the very first day, that she was the coldest woman he'd ever met? For the first time, as she kept her eyes anxiously fixed on the table top, as she felt tears beginning to threaten, Carrie faced the awful truth that she was, in far too many ways, just what Zachary had called her that day, cold and unfeeling. What a dreadful, dreadful thing to have to face about oneself!

"Carrie, honey, would you like to dance?" Mark asked her, his hand touching her arm. As her eyes darted up, Carrie saw that Zachary and Linda were standing, and with friendly smiles were excusing themselves to go to the dance floor. That was the final straw—tears flooded into Carrie's eyes that she seemed powerless to blink back.

"No, Mark. Thank you, but no thanks. I—I think I'd better go to the ladies' room." Pushing her chair awkwardly back, Carrie jumped up and hurriedly fled.

By the time she returned to the table a few minutes later, she had gotten herself under control. She had lectured herself, staring at herself in a full-length mirror in the ladies' room, that there was not a single thing wrong with her dress. The fact was that it was a very flattering one, and always had been, the fit of it showing off to perfection her slender, gracefully curved figure—and when Zachary had first seen her, there had been nothing fraudulent about the way his eyes had lit up with pleasure. A well-cut dress, like this one, stayed in fashion year after year. In addition, the pale gray color, with a light-shimmering, almost lavender cast to it, was the most becoming color she'd ever worn, seeming to light up her wide gray eyes and setting off the pink of her rather pale face. Looking at herself from every angle in the mirror, Carrie felt her heart bouncing back up, and soon concluded that there was nothing about her appearance which need make her the least self-conscious. In any case, appearance was only appearance, and for heaven's sake tonight wasn't a contest to see which woman in the room had on the prettiest dress. So Linda was wearing a truly spectacular gown, so what? *I look just fine*, Carrie told herself, and squared back her shoulders to venture back out.

And as for the fact Linda was a prettier woman than she was, again so what? Many, many women were far more beautiful than she was—was she going to let that spoil her life? It had never upset her before and most certainly shouldn't now. A pretty face was not what counted; rather what lived behind the pretty face was the crucial issue. And if *I don't like what I see when I look into myself*, Carrie scolded herself, then the thing to do about that is not to sulk or fall into despair, but to change. If I truly admire the warm friendliness of a woman like Linda, then it's time I learned to be more warm and friendly myself. For now, however, the main thing was to walk back out there, chin up, shoulders back, and show the world she could handle herself, that she was a self-composed, mature woman capable of maintaining her poise no matter how unsettling the situation in which she found herself.

When she arrived back at the table, both men rising with appreciative glances her way, Linda smiling warmly at her, Carrie found that a discussion was now under way as to the Wilderness Areas Bill. But though Mark and Zachary were openly acknowledged opponents on the merits of the bill, Carrie realized with intense relief that they were discussing it with courteous, calm rationality. When the waiter arrived at their table, order pad in hand, the discussion was dropped for a time as they all checked their menus and ordered dinner, but once that necessary business was out of the way and the waiter left, the discussion of the Wilderness Areas Bill was immediately resumed.

"Certainly we're all well aware that a bill of some kind, preserving some of Alaska's vast underdeveloped areas for national parks and wilderness areas, is going to go through in time," Zachary commented, frowning across the table at Mark, "but as I understand it, the question is still up for grabs as to the extent of land that will be involved. The Udall bill, which Carrie told me you're working to have pass, as I understand it, would set off approximately one-fourth of the state, which many of us, the governor included, feel is a bit too much."

Zachary suddenly grinned, adding, "As Governor Hammond said, Alaska certainly recognizes that the entire nation has a stake in this area. All the Alaskans ask is that the national government not try to drive that stake through Alaska's heart."

This quote from the governor brought a slight tense smile to Mark's lips, and a brief little laugh. Carrie tensed slightly for an instant, but the next moment relaxed again as it became evident that Mark was not going to rush in angrily to rebut the governor's position.

The grin on Zachary's face died away. He shifted a bit on his chair, and said, in a deep earnest voice to Mark, "But the truth is, Mark, I've only been in this area a couple of years, as possibly you know, and during that time I've been exploring almost continuously up in the north slope area, so I haven't had the chance to familiarize myself with the various proposals as thoroughly as I would have liked. I know that you and most environmentalists favor the Udall bill, also that former Secretary of the Interior Rogers Morton proposed a bill, and also that there's a third bill sponsored by Senator Stevens and backed by Governor Hammond, but that's about the extent of my familiarity with the problem. I'm not at all up on the details of the various bills. Possibly you could fill me in?"

Carrie saw the immediate gleam of pleasure come into Mark's eyes at this chance to expound on his favorite subject, and for the next two hours, as they ate dinner and then lingered over their after-dinner coffee, Mark held forth, detailing, and explaining, the various controversial bills. As Carrie sat quietly watching Mark, she knew without question that he was thoroughly enjoying himself, and Zachary, an apparently deeply appreciative listener, seemed also to be highly pleased at the turn the evening had taken. Occasionally glancing across at Linda, who kept her eyes fixed on Mark's face and who quite often broke in to ask surprisingly perceptive, informed questions, Carrie was forced to the conclusion that Linda too was thoroughly engrossed and entertained. In fact, Carrie realized in time, stiffling a little sigh, she seemed to be the only one who was less than thrilled by Mark's informative lecture, no doubt because it was far from new to her; she had heard it all numerous times before.

As she picked rather listlessly at her dinner, trying to enjoy it, Carrie felt herself sink again into a mood of tearful despair. As hard as she tried to fight this down, the contrast between the two men she sat between, Mark and Zachary, began to weigh on her more and more. Mark was doing all the talking, therefore should certainly have seemed the more alive and vital, yet somehow even with this advantage he didn't. Even the animation of his face as he talked seemed superficial and empty somehow; the fire in his eyes lifeless.

All Zachary was doing, in contrast, was sitting quietly listening, rarely moving, rarely interjecting even a word, but in spite of this his vibrant vitality remained such a powerful force, it seemed to Carrie, that it reached out and enveloped everyone there. Somehow he reduced Mark, with his handsome young face and pale blue eyes, to little more than an animated puppet, gabbing away with no real life or force of his own. The few times that Carrie dared glance directly at Zachary, her heart immediately ached. Once, when she glanced around and Zachary, noticing, turned his eyes to meet hers, the force of his gaze seemed to cut through her like an electric shock, zinging along each nerve. After that she did not risk looking his way again.

While Zachary, in his radiant male vitality, seemed to reduce Mark to a shallow and empty boy, it seemed to Carrie that Linda Grant, seated across the table from her with that eager, absorbed look on her face, her lovely brown eyes lustrously gleaming, did even worse things to her, Carrie, aging her, depleting her, turning her into a thin, gray, pale-eyed specter. This perception brought on the most depressing thought of all: that while Zachary and Linda, in their warm, vibrant aliveness, belonged together and deserved each other, the same was true of her and Mark; in their dead, empty shallowness they belonged together too, deserved each other too. No wonder she had always felt so ill at ease with Zachary, so frightened of him. With Zachary she was completely out of her element, her natural mate being a man like Mark.

At last Mark wound down, bringing his lecture to a close. With a smug, happy little smile, he reached for his water glass and took a long drink. Zachary, with a sudden grin, sat forward and said, "Well, I truly thank you, Mark. You've cleared up a great many questions I had and I can't tell you how much I've enjoyed it. Thank you so much."

"The same goes for me," Linda said, with a warm, sweet smile. "You really clarified a complex subject and made it just fascinating. I don't know when I've enjoyed any evening so much." Linda's eyes swung around to Carrie's face. "Hopefully, Carrie, you enjoyed it too?"

Carrie smiled rather shyly, shrugging. "Well, yes, I did, though the truth is, Linda, I've heard it all a few times before."

Linda burst out with a soft, sympathetic laugh. "Poor Carrie, I imagine you have, at that. Well, the least we can do is give your fiancé back to you now." Turning to Zachary, she touched his arm. "Come on, Zack, let's go dance."

Zachary stood up at once, helped Linda up, and they left to walk to the dance floor. Mark's eyes followed them as they left, then he turned to face Carrie, the same smug, satisfied look around his mouth.

With a spurt of dislike at that look, Carrie commented, a dry edge to her voice, "I thought the idea of spending the evening with Zachary tonight was that you were going to pump him for his ideas, rather than the other way around."

A slightly startled look crossed through Mark's eyes, then with a self-satisfied little laugh he pressed his hand over hers on the table top. "Well, the best one can do is scatter a few seeds around and hope a few fall on fertile ground," Mark responded rather pompously. "I know you've heard it all before, so naturally you were bound to feel a little bit bored, but—" He shrugged away the rest of the sentence, smiling at her.

Tensing with irritation Carrie said, her voice edged with sharpness, "You don't for one minute think you altered Zachary's opinion on the Udall bill by anything you said?" though her cheeks flushed with regret even as she said this. The last thing she wanted was to start a fight with Mark here and now, in public, with Zachary and Linda due to rejoin them any moment.

Feeling ashamed of herself for needling him, Carrie was intensely relieved to hear Mark laugh in response, obviously unwilling to take offense. His hand continued to press on hers, his eyes moving out to the dance floor.

"Curtis isn't a bad guy," he murmured thoughtfully a moment later. "Of course I still think he's got one hell of a nerve, moving into our state and immediately arranging to throw his money and weight around on a crucial state issue, but that's only to be expected of a man like that, one who races around the world exploiting the earth for all he's worth, just to make himself rich—the greedy, exploitive bastard."

As she sat staring out at the dance floor, Carrie's eyes caught Zachary and Linda dancing. She bit at her lip, then snapped furiously in answer, "So what's so terribly wrong about spending your life exploring for new energy sources? Even your mother concedes we are unquestionably caught up in an energy crunch which can only get worse. If something isn't done, our whole industrial way of life will grind to a halt, with millions of people being thrown out of work, bringing untold misery. Is that what you're so eager to see?"

Eyes blazing with anger, Carrie turned to glare at Mark, and with instant relief saw again that he was in too good a humor to take offense. Instead he laughed softly, squeezing her hand even harder under his.

"Okay, honey, okay," he said soothingly, and laughed briefly again. "Curtis, or someone, has sure gotten through to you, to where you scarcely sound like yourself anymore. Of course we face an energy problem, but—oh, hell," Mark suddenly interrupted himself, "let's not fight it out tonight, all right? Want to dance?"

After a very brief hesitation, Carrie murmured, "All right, fine," and as Mark stood up she did, too, and allowed herself to be led to the dance floor.

As she and Mark began dancing, Carrie's eyes happened on Zachary and Linda again, and momentarily her heart seemed to stop at what a lovely, well-matched couple they made, Zachary so tall, broad and powerful in appearance, Linda slender, willowy, graceful, held with such seeming tenderness and affection in the circle of Zachary's arm. Seeing them made Carrie feel instantly thin, gray, colorless and old again, and in a mood of lonely despondency she pressed up against Mark, grateful for the protective warmth of his arm around her.

"Linda's a warm, lovely young woman, isn't she?" Carrie murmured, as though if she put this assessment into words it might hurt just a slight bit less.

Mark's eyes circled around as though to refresh his memory of what Linda Grant looked like. "Not bad," he responded, in a coolly indifferent tone. "But that's the way it is with wealthy men like Curtis, they can buy the best there is on the market. They don't have to settle for anything less."

Instantly angered, Carrie drew back, gray eyes blazing. "What a lousy, slanderous thing to say!" she snapped. "You don't have a reason in the world to suppose she's not genuinely fond of him. Is every woman in the world up for sale, is that what you think?" She couldn't remember ever feeling so furious at him before.

"Hey, calm down, sweetie, for Pete's sake," Mark responded, laughing, drawing her stiff, angry body close again. He danced a few awkward steps, then whispered good humoredly into her ear, "What's the matter with you anyway? Every damn word I say you take offense at. Obviously you're spoiling for a fight, as I was the other night." He drew back a bit then, his eyes gazing steadily into hers. "So what's really bugging you, Carrie? Out with it, all right?"

Mark stopped moving, and Carrie did too. They stood on the dance floor, his arm still around her, while Carrie did her best to look directly into his eyes, fresh despair pouring through her. *Oh, Mark, I don't know,* she wanted to cry out, *I just don't know what's the matter with me! I'm not sure I love you anymore, if I ever did; I'm just not sure about anything anymore—except that right at the moment I need you so much!*

Stepping up close again, pressing against him, Carrie said quickly, furiously blinking against her tears, "Mark, I'm sorry. Let's just dance again, all right?"

Mark nodded, and holding her close began dancing again, while Carrie told herself that everything was all right, everything was fine, or if not fine now, once she got her head back together again it would be fine. Once this dreadful evening drew to a close . . .

A few minutes later, as she and Mark started off the floor, Zachary walked over with Linda, suggesting with a smile that they switch partners for one dance. Carrie instinctively tensed, wanting to refuse, to run and hide, but there seemed to be no decent way out of it, and the next thing she knew, Zachary's arm was firmly around her and he was dancing her off.

At first they just danced, Zachary not speaking, and Carrie felt enormously grateful. For the first few steps she felt so stiff and tense she all but tripped over her own feet, but slowly, as she got to where she could breathe more easily again, she began to relax, to allow Zachary to guide her, to move rhythmically with him to the music. Closing her eyes, she found herself visualizing how she must look in Zachary's arms. In this way, possibly, she could drive out all memory of how Linda Grant had looked!

The piece drew to a close and still Zachary had not spoken to her. As they stopped moving, Carrie reopened her eyes. Glancing up into Zachary's face, she felt fresh lightning rip down through her to find his dark eyes fixed piercingly down on her.

"Your friend Linda is a—a very lovely young woman," she stuttered out, unwilling to face how desperately her heart ached that moment for reassurance.

"Yes, she certainly is," Zachary responded, unsmiling. "She's the daughter of a close friend of mine, a man I've had business dealings with for fifteen years, so I've known Linda since she was five. Currently she's a college student, majoring in ecology, intensely interested in the very same things that you and Mark are, the various wilderness areas bills, which is why I invited her along tonight."

Zachary paused momentarily, then, as the music started up again, he put his arm around her, drew her close, and, staring fixedly down at her, remarked rather irritably, "Carrie, you're the woman I'm in love with, the only one, the woman I'm still determined to marry," after which he said no more as he whirled her off across the floor.

With Zachary's frightening words echoing and re-echoing in her head, Carrie's heart beat so hard and fast she was afraid she might faint. She feared that her trembling limbs might fly off, or her legs give out from under her. *Oh, Zack, don't!* Carrie thought in acute distress, tears threatening to overflow her eyes. *I just can't handle it, so please don't say that, just leave me alone!* If only this dance would come to an end!

At last it did, and without saying anything more except to thank her, Zachary led her back to the table. Without reseating herself, Carrie suggested to Mark, trying desperately to speak in a calm and steady voice, that she was feeling rather tired and it seemed to her it was time to leave.

A surprised, displeased look appeared in Mark's eyes, but a moment later he stood up and replied in gentlemanly fashion that of course if she wished to go home now, they would. He stepped around the table to shake hands with Zachary, each man again expressing pleasure at their chance to spend the evening together, then Mark smiled at Linda, saying good-night to her. The next moment Mark was leading her out, Carrie walking stiffly, head high, eyes staring straight ahead, as she tried to repress all memory of the one glance she'd gotten of Zachary's face, his eyes flashing at her in hotly contemptuous reproach that once again she was running from him, running away.

You just can't stand up to any emotion, can you? his piercing dark eyes had snapped at her. *You're still frozen inside, as frozen as the Arctic itself, still the coldest human being I've ever known.*

Fighting back tears, Carrie walked hurriedly alongside Mark out of the restaurant and out to his car. During the evening Zachary had mentioned that his explorations for natural gas reserves in the north slope area were about to wind up, that he would only be in the area for a few more weeks, then would take off for his next project, drilling for oil in Mexico, so before long he would be gone, she wouldn't have to face him or his scathing contempt anymore.

I can't help it, Zack, if I just can't return your love! Carrie defended herself frantically in her thoughts, but even in her own ears the defense sounded weak and sniveling, fully deserving of the contempt Zachary's eyes had showered on her. As Mark drove them home, still with the same happy, self-satisfied flush on his cheeks, Carrie rested her head back, closing her eyes, telling herself that Zachary hadn't really meant what he'd said. Over the past few months he had merely found her an entertaining challenge, had merely set out to prove that no woman could resist him, that he could even win over a woman with a heart as cold and unfeeling as hers was. What better way to while away one's spare time in the frozen north?

Once they'd arrived home, Carrie said a quick goodnight to Mark's parents, who were still up watching television, then she hurried up to her bedroom, deeply relieved to be alone again at last, to be able to crawl despondently into bed and shut out the world.

Oh, Zack, dammit, why did you have to come along and do this to me? her heart moaned angrily. Though she yanked over the thin, lavender-scented pillow and held it pressed down over her head, still she refused to let go and give in to tears. If only she could shut out Zack's voice telling her she was the only woman he loved; even more importantly, shut out the withering look of contempt he had given her for once again running away. Oh, dammit, dammit, anyway!

Thankfully, it would all soon be over. She'd be back at her clinic in Point Hope, busily at work, free of Mark, and within a couple of weeks Zachary would be gone, off to Mexico, he had said, in search of new ways to despoil the earth. *Oh, Zack, I just couldn't let you despoil and destroy me too!* Carrie defended herself hotly, insistently screaming this at Zack in her thoughts, until at last she drifted off into a restless, unhappy sleep.

CHAPTER 10

Two days later Carrie flew black to Point Hope. She was accompanied by Mark, who planned to spend a couple of days with her, through New Year's, before returning to his job in Washington.

Long before boarding the plane to fly back to the clinic, Carrie had calmed down, accepting again with equanimity her engagement to Mark and her choice of a future as his wife. Zachary's passionate responses to life, his compelling vitality, were too rich for her blood, too shattering to her nerves, besides which she still didn't trust the man, still felt that he must be playing some cat-and-mouse game with her. Let him leave the Arctic area within a few weeks as planned; truthfully, she'd be glad to see the last of him, glad to have him gone once and for all. His longed-for departure would restore welcome peace to her mind and her heart. She could go back to being the self-contained, poised, self-sufficient woman she had been before his disruptive intrusion into her life.

As she showed Mark around the small village which

had long before then become very dear to her, she could tell that, while he was doing his best to act interested and entertained, he was in truth terribly bored. Mark felt no natural interest in people, had no natural warmth to offer others Carrie suddenly realized, watching his stiff little smile as she introduced him to villagers she had gotten to know. How could she have failed to notice before how cold and distant his manner was?

She had arranged for Mark to spend his nights in the village "hotel," where tourists were put up during the summer months. Walking back to her clinic after leaving him there, Carrie felt lonely and upset. She kept remembering the day she'd taken Zachary on a tour of the village. Though he'd been unusually quiet and reserved that day, for him, nevertheless she had sensed his genuine interest in everything they saw, a warm and genuine *caring*, while Mark's cold, bored indifference today . . .

Did Mark truly have no concern for anything outside himself, was he totally self-absorbed? Pondering this question, Carrie remembered a wisecrack she'd once heard about a famous liberal politician, that the man's passionate love for mankind was equaled only by his cold dislike of people. The same thing could be said of Mark, couldn't it? Or, to paraphrase it, his passionate concern for the rights of unborn generations was equaled only by his utterly cold indifference to the rights of those already living. If fresh supplies of energy, like the natural gas Zachary's company was exploring for, weren't found, and the entire industrial behemoth of western civilization ground to a halt, destroying millions of lives, Mark's smug response would be, "So what?" As long as the earth was "protected" for those generations not yet born, Mark couldn't care less about what happened to those already struggling through life. *He would even enjoy the thought of all that suffering,* Carrie thought suddenly, *smug, self-satisfied sadist that he is!*

Shocked at this thought, Carrie quickly fought it down, telling herself she was overly tired, that was the only reason she was being so harsh on Mark. Actually the whole question of "progress" versus environmental protection was such a complex one, touching upon such a wide variety of important issues, it was no wonder it seemed impossible to arrive at a just and humane solution. Mark was no more wrong than anyone else; possibly, also, he was no more right. So let the problem stay where it was, Carrie decided, in the hands of the bureaucrats, the politicians, and the voters, and let them wrestle and wrangle their way to a solution as best they could. She was tired of even thinking about it.

Reaching her clinic, she walked wearily up the steps. For hours today she'd had to face what a cold and distant nature Mark had, how icily unfriendly he was, but wasn't that true of her too? Wasn't that why she had never really noticed it in him before? Her head suddenly beating with pain, Carrie raised a hand to press it hard against her forehead. Face it, she thought, for no matter how it hurt, it was true. In some ways she had the same lofty and impersonal nature that Mark had. She'd gone into medicine not only because it allowed her to devote herself to others, as Mark was "devoting" himself to environmentalist causes, but also because in medicine she could remain distant, reserved, uninvolved with people. As a doctor she was not expected to get emotionally attached to her patients; in fact, throughout her training she had been repeatedly warned not to do so. That aloofness, that lack of involvement, a doctor's professionally detached, clinical attitude—wasn't that one of the things about medicine that had most attracted her?

Of course it was! So she had no basis upon which to criticize Mark for being what he was, her natural counterpart, her ideal mate. They were two cold, aloof people who had happily accepted a cold, aloof engagement, and one day they would marry and adjust perfectly to a cold, bored marriage. Just as they had nothing to offer other people, they had nothing to offer each other either. A perfect pairing.

Carrie went into her living quarters, quickly undressed, and climbed into bed, but then found she couldn't sleep. She could see clearly now that Mark, for all his years of "devotion" to her, was quite incapable of loving anyone. But she had no right to complain about this, for if Zachary had taught her one thing about herself, it was that she too was incapable of loving. Fortunately, she and Mark had already decided that they wouldn't have children. Mark had explained his lack of desire for children by stating emphatically that with the world in such deplorable shape, it was doing a grave injustice to a child to cause him to be born, an argument she had accepted without the slightest protest. Her own feeling had been that, as she wanted to devote herself to mankind through medicine, having a child would be disruptive and foolish; surely she could do more general good in the world if she didn't tie herself down with children.

Oh, what lovely, lofty excuses we gave ourselves! Carrie thought now, lying on her back in her narrow bed, staring up at the low ceiling. Neither she nor Mark was capable of giving genuine love to anyone. Neither had an ounce of love in his heart to give. So they'd naturally gravitated to each other and had come up with high-sounding reasons not to bring forth a child whose need for love they would never have been able to meet.

Well, no matter what reasons we gave each other, at least we knew ourselves well enough to know we didn't have it in us to be loving parents, Carrie thought. But instead of soothing her, this thought made her feel even worse, even more empty and dead inside. Suddenly her arms felt so lonely, lonely to hold someone she loved, a man she loved, a baby she loved. How could she spend—waste—her whole life without ever holding close to her someone she loved?

She lay for a long time pondering this, staring into the cold, empty, loveless future she saw for herself, before she was finally able to close her eyes and drift off into a restless sleep.

In the morning she slept late, was awakened at last by a pounding on the door to her room.

"Carrie, honey, wake up. It's me, Mark. May I come in?"

Carrie struggled to sit up, tried to force her sore, sleep-drugged eyes to stay open and called back hoarsely, "Mark? Just a minute, please." She threw herself out of bed, grabbed for her robe and pulled it on, switched on the light, then walked unsteadily over toward the washbasin on the sink, calling out, "All right, Mark, come on in." What was he doing here so blasted early?

Mark stepped in with an amused smile rippling across his mouth. Glancing around at him, Carrie noticed, with a slight trip of her pulse, that his handsome young face looked almost radiant, more aglow than she'd ever known it to look, and his blue eyes danced. He strode rapidly across to her, threw his arms around her waist, and pressed a kiss against the base of her throat. Today he did not seem at all the cold, bored, bloodless man he had seemed the day before, the smug, self-absorbed creature she had decided was incapable of love. Perhaps, being tired and upset, she had misjudged both Mark and herself. But what in the world had put him in such high spirits?

Carrie broke free of his hold, murmuring that she had to wash, had to dress, and Mark stepped away, laughing.

"Guess what, sweetheart? I've been lying awake in bed for hours, impatiently waiting for the sun to rise, before it finally broke through my thick skull where I was, clear up here in the godforsaken Arctic, farther north than I've ever been before, the land of perpetual night."

Mark laughed a brief, delighted laugh. "I've been down in Washington for so long now, where the sun behaves as it should, that I just never gave any thought to what you've been putting up with up here, a summer day that's months long with the sun never setting, then the long Arctic night when the sun comes up at twelve noon and sets again one minute later. How in the world did you ever adjust to it?"

"Oh, it's not as bad as all that," Carrie murmured defensively, pouring the water she had heated into her large bowl to wash. "And from now on the days will be getting longer and longer."

Mark shook his head in good-natured wonderment. "You know, Carrie, I've heard it said all my life that the Eskimos are as hardy a breed of men as ever lived, and, by God, it must be true, not only to put up with the brutal cold up here and the terrible isolation, but to be able to adjust to the weird behavior of the sun."

"Well—I suppose people can get used to anything," Carrie murmured anxiously, disconcerted over this fresh, amused, glowing Mark right after she had pigeonholed him forever as without life, without heart. She turned around abruptly to face him. "Look, Mark, I'm really not ready for company so soon after getting up. Why don't you go into my living room and give me a chance to wash and dress?"

"All right, pumpkin," Mark agreed goodnaturedly. That was the first time he had ever called her that, or, indeed, any oddball endearment. "Whatever you say. This is the last day of the old year, you know, and the last thing I want is to discomfort you in any way." With a friendly smile, he left.

In less than fifteen minutes Carrie was washed, coiffed, dressed, and she and Mark were walking to the village coffee shop for breakfast. Carrie felt mildly depressed, feeling that the night before, in foreseeing such a bleak future, she had made a fool of herself. So Mark had felt tired and dispirited the day before. For heaven's sake, everyone had a right to an off day once in a while! And the way she had made a federal case out of it . . .

"You know, Mark," she remarked suddenly, not knowing she was going to say this, "I've been giving some thought to the agreement we made not to have children. I mean, the older I get—" Her voice died away.

Mark took hold of her arm. "Honey, I know what you mean," he said. "The older I get, the more I debate the whole question, too, wondering whether we weren't too young to decide such a profoundly important issue when we did decide it. But after all," he threw in cheerfully, his face brightening with a quick smile, "it's not as though the decision we made was irrevocable, not subject to later revision if we so decide. Once we get married—well, let's agree right now that the whole question of whether or not we'll have a family is again open to question and debate. All right?"

Mark stopped walking to face her, his light blue eyes meeting hers, and after a slight hesitation Carrie nodded in agreement, doing her best to fight down a slight stinging mist that rose to her eyes. With Mark being so warm and friendly this morning, so tender and understanding . . .

As his smile faded away, Mark added as they started walking again, "At the same time, in all truth, Carrie, I haven't yet quite persuaded myself that having a child, considering the deplorable state the world is in today, isn't a truly heinous crime. But naturally even that doesn't quite kill off the instinctive urge I have, deep inside, to perpetuate myself by bringing forth new life, the one sure immortality we have."

Carrie listened with dismay in her heart. How cool and logical Mark's reaction was compared to Zachary's, Zack who had said at once that of course he was going to have children, the more the merrier! But she'd already faced that she couldn't handle Zack, with his excessive exuberance for life, his overpowering vitality, his aggressive masculinity, and that was that. She belonged with Mark, who would never ask too much of her, or expect too great closeness, or try to draw from her a love that was foreign to her nature, which would threaten her very being. As to whether or not she and Mark decided in the future to have a child—well, that certainly didn't have to be decided today.

A heavy resignation sank through her and Carrie glanced around at Mark, forcing out a smile, doing her best to adjust to her fate. This was her man, her proper mate. In time they would marry and surely it would all work out. All memory of Zachary Curtis would fade away like a vivid but frightening dream, to trouble her no more.

They were having a hot, appetizing breakfast of scrambled eggs and ham, and were conversing amiably when they first heard the news. One of the men from the En-Ex camp a few miles away stopped at their table to tell them. Zachary and Matt Sanders were hours overdue from their flight back from Anchorage. They had stopped over at Fairbanks, then had departed from Fairbanks the day before, and should have arrived over twelve hours earlier. Their radio contact with the camp had ceased suddenly about three the previous afternoon, and no word had been heard from them since.

"Oh, my God," Carrie moaned, one of her hands flying immediately to her mouth, pressing against it.

"How dreadful," Mark murmured, his eyes caught on the other man's face. "How much longer will you wait before you set up a search party?"

The man standing beside their table, a tall, heavyset, middle-aged man with a wide gap between his large, stained teeth shook his head in distress. Carrie had met this man, Otto Ranklin, once before.

"We alerted the authorities hours ago, not long after radio contact ended, but so far we haven't gotten very far. We're flying up another company plane which should get here late today and we'll begin our own search with that. But how far are we apt to get even if we could line up every airplane in the state to go out looking? When you consider the vastness of the area ... Well, I thought you might want to know," he muttered, and strode off.

Carrie tried to take another bite of egg but found she couldn't. With a trembling hand she reached for her cup and sipped her coffee. Zachary—Zachary and

Matt . . . Oh, she couldn't believe that they wouldn't make it safely back!

"Want to go?" Mark asked her gently, reaching over to touch her arm. "Obviously we've both lost our appetite and might as well admit it. Surely the next news we'll get is that Curtis has made it through safely after all, in spite of the loss of radio contact. In any case, there's little point in our worrying about it, which won't help them one bit."

"Maybe not," Carrie tried to say, lifting her hurting eyes, "but that doesn't mean . . ." She couldn't go on. How did one keep from worrying faced with news like that?

They left the coffee shop and began walking slowly, aimlessly, back toward the clinic. While they'd been inside eating, the sun had risen palely into the sky. Surely, now that it was daylight . . . But, as Otto Ranklin had said, when you thought of the vastness of the area, the towering peaks of the Brooks Range which jutted up between Fairbanks and here—how could anyone suppose that search planes would have the least chance of spotting one tiny downed plane?

As tears filled her eyes, Carrie turned to Mark, resting her head against him. "Oh, Mark, I'm just so worried—"

"Of course you are, sweetheart," Mark responded, putting both arms around her and drawing her close. "After all, in the months you've been here you've gotten to know the man—both men—so no matter what your feelings toward them are, you're bound to feel worried now."

Mark let go of her, then put his mittened hands along her cheeks to lift her face to where his eyes could meet hers.

"But, Carrie," he said quietly but urgently, "don't

let your worry get out of hand, all right? This is the thirty-first, you know, tonight's New Year's Eve, and tomorrow I have to leave to return to Washington. So let's not let this spoil our last day together, especially when you stop to realize it may be a very long time before we'll get to see each other again."

"All—all right, Mark," Carrie agreed, her voice all but breaking, "at least I'll try. But when you think about what Otto said—"

Mark, smiling, put a hand to her lips. "So don't think about it," he insisted cheerfully. "After all, what does it really mean to us? This kind of thing happens every day. Accidents happen, planes go down, people die. But neither one of us has the least control over that. What we *do* have control over is how we are going to react, and I say the only sensible thing is simply to push the thought of it out of our minds. Agreed?"

Carrie lifted her hand to push Mark's finger away from her mouth. "I can't believe what I'm hearing," she said, anger coming to her rescue to lighten the weight of her worry. "You heard what Otto said. Can't you pretend that you *care*? This is a man you met and spent an enjoyable evening with just a few nights ago, and even if that weren't so, even if you'd never met him . . . Oh, Mark, what kind of a monster are you anyway? Don't you care at all?"

"The kind of monster I am," Mark snapped in answer, "is that I'm not a hypocrite. I'm not about to pretend, even to you, especially to you, that I care about someone I don't care about. So I met the man once, what does that mean? I didn't like him, didn't agree with him. As you know, he's pitting money and prestige against everything I believe in, so if you think I'm going to put on a display of phony grief if

177

it turns out his plane has gone down and he's removed from the scene, you can think again. As far as I'm concerned, his death leaves me with one less opponent I need worry about."

Carrie's tears seemed to dry up as she stared in horror, her eyes caught on Mark's light blue ones. The first day she'd met Zachary he'd accused her of being inhumanly cold and hostile. Now, staring into Mark's coolly angry blue eyes, she saw the heartless hostility that Zachary had meant. Mark truly did not care, did not care whether or not Zachary and Matt had crashed and now lay dead or dying; in fact, he no doubt secretly wished that they had. One less enemy for him to have to worry about. Except for a small tight clique—his parents, her, a few close friends—every living being was an enemy to Mark, Carrie suddenly realized.

Am I like that too? Carrie asked herself. *Oh, I'm not, I'm not!* Fresh tears rose and quickly overflowed, tears of worry over Zachary and Matt, yet tears of relief, too, relief that she could care enough to cry, to feel as though her heart was going to break. Zachary and Matt *had* to make it safely back!

"Mark, I'm sorry but I don't want to spend any more time with you," Carrie murmured, and brushing past him she walked rapidly away. She feared for a moment that Mark would come racing after her, that he'd confront her, try to reason with her, win her back, but he didn't. After she'd gotten close to fifty yards away, Carrie glanced back once, quickly, and saw that Mark stood right where she'd left him, staring after her, but he hadn't taken a single step to follow her, thankfully.

She returned to her clinic and found she had two

patients waiting. She tried to get her mind off the dreadful news she'd heard long enough to minister to them.

That afternoon Mark came to the clinic looking pale and troubled. Carrie found herself able to face him with remarkable calm, without the least trace of anger, and able to say at last, without hesitation or equivocation, the words that had been forming inside her all that week.

"Mark, we've known each other for a very long time, and in many ways I feel deeply grateful to you, and very fond of you, but I have definitely decided that I no longer wish to marry you. Therefore, I want you to take your ring back—" she picked it up from the table top where she had placed it earlier after slipping it off, "—and to consider our engagement off. I'm sorry if this upsets you, truly sorry, but my mind is definitely made up and I know I won't change it. So please take your ring."

As she held it out, Mark waited a moment or two, then with a sigh lifted a hand and allowed her to drop the ring into it. He stood gazing steadily down at where it lay in the palm of his hand, then his eyes came up to meet hers as a nervous smile struggled across his mouth.

"Isn't this going a bit too far? Overreacting? Just because you're feeling upset right now, and somewhat worried . . . Look, Carrie, I'm sorry I didn't react the way you wanted me to about Curtis and his overdue plane, but you don't really want me to be a hypocrite, do you? I'm sure that once you've given yourself a day or two to think things over, you'll see that I'm right."

Mark's smile broadened as he held the ring back out. "Once you've calmed down and gotten over your anger at me, I know you'll regret this, so why don't you be the sensible person I know you are and take this back right now?"

"No, Mark, I won't," Carrie said quickly, shaking her head as she backed away. "I know I'll never regret what I'm doing, and I don't need any time to think it over. I've had lots of time to consider this, ever since last July, in fact, and I've decided at last that, just like you, I don't want to be a hypocrite.

"The reason I can't marry you, Mark, is that I no longer love you, if I ever did." She paused long enough to take a deep breath, then managed to get out the frightening words, "For the fact is I've fallen in love with someone else, fallen deeply in love, and—and for that reason alone there is no possible chance I'll ever change my mind."

"You've fallen in love with another man?" Mark echoed dubiously. "Carrie, I don't believe you. Isolated up here, cut off from everyone—what man?" he demanded to know.

Though her cheeks burned uncomfortably, Carrie managed to look directly at Mark as she answered, "You know what man. Apparently you suspected it right along. Zachary Curtis."

"Curtis?" Mark repeated in disbelief. His cheeks flushing red, he burst out laughing. "Oh, I can't believe that! You and Curtis—God, Carrie, how absurd! Can't you see how absurd that is?"

Tensing, trembling, Carrie snapped, "Mark, that's enough. Please just go. I don't want to discuss it anymore."

"Of course not!" Mark mocked, forcing out another laugh. "It's too ludicrous even to discuss. You saw the type of woman Curtis likes, young, sexy, gorgeous, the kind he can get any time simply with a snap of the finger. And now you're ready to throw me over for a man you don't stand a chance in hell of winning!"

"Will you please just go?" Carrie cried. "Just get out! I don't want to hear another word!"

Swinging away, Mark spat out sarcastically, "With his plane a day overdue, he's probably dead at this point anyway. If it turns out he is, just don't change your mind and come crawling back to me!"

He opened the door and was through it before Carrie could scream out after him, "Don't worry, I won't!" As Mark closed the waiting room door, leaving Carrie alone, she lowered her head as tears rose up and overflowed, as she shook from head to toe with the force of her sobs. Zachary had said once that he was going to melt her heart. Surely he had succeeded, for a heart that was cold and frozen couldn't possibly hurt as hers did. *Oh, Zachary,* she thought, *you mustn't be dead!*

Sometime later the door opened, an Eskimo woman stepping in with a broad shy smile, and Carrie hastily fought down her sobs, dried her tears, and turned her attention to her patient. Surely she would soon receive word that Zachary's plane had arrived safely after all.

But no word came, and after her patient left, Carrie closed up and hurried down to the village to hear if there was any further news. There wasn't. On impulse, as she walked worriedly back toward the clinic, she turned and went out to the airstrip instead, telling herself not to despair, not to let grief overtake her. Zachary was too full of life, far too vibrant, not to be still alive. Any minute now his plane would come into view overhead, easing down . . .

As she thought this, repeatedly closing her eyes, attempting to make it happen by sheer force of will, Carrie heard the distant but distinct whirr of a motor, and as her eyes opened, she cried out in joy. There *was* a plane coming in, and, as it dipped in lower, she could make out the markings on the side. En-Ex. The plane she'd prayed it would be, Zachary's company plane!

With a whoop of joy, her heart bounding up, Carrie burst into a run toward the strip, every fiber of her being crying out in relief. The plane hadn't crashed after all, Zachary and Matt were all right! As she ran forward, blinded by her tears, she lost traction once, falling down, sprawling and sliding on the ice, but she scrambled up at once again to run even faster. The plane had just touched down as she reached the strip; she ran forward with her arms hungrily aching to be thrown around the man she had so recently feared was dead. As she came up along the side of the plane, panting, her lungs hurt from her breathlessness but never had her heart felt so full, so alive, so happy. The man piloting the plane climbed out and Carrie ran the last few yards, wanting nothing more than to throw herself against him and never leave his arms again.

Then she caught her first glimpse of the man's face and in shock saw that it wasn't Zachary.

Her step faltered, stopped, and she stared in confusion, panting, still not able to believe her eyes. This *was* the En-Ex plane, the one in which Zachary had taken her up for that lovely scenic flight. How could the man who had climbed out not be Zachary? The pilot, noticing her there, took her arm and drew her away from the airstrip.

"Any word yet?" he asked her, as though she would be the source of information she had hoped he would be. In mounting confusion Carrie shook her head, grief and despair rising in her so fast they threatened to overwhelm her. Now she remembered what Otto Ranklin had told her and Mark in the coffee shop that morning. The company was flying in its second plane to begin search operations for the one in which Zachary and Matt were now presumed to have crashed. But everyone knew that a search operation in this vast, frozen, uninhabited region was little more than a meaningless gesture. A plane downed in the Brooks Range had about as much chance of being located and recovered as a drop of water splashed into the ocean had. *But I mustn't give up hope!* Carrie told herself, knowing that it was going to be almost impossible not to.

New Year's Eve. A night of anxiety and grief such as Carrie had never known before. A night in which she used every ounce of energy she had to keep herself buoyed up one level above complete despair. Mark came by the clinic early that evening, asking to talk to her, and in her loneliness and grief Carrie was glad to see him.

After each had apologized for the angry words that morning, they sat in her little sitting room for another two hours with little to say to each other. Then Mark kissed her good-night on the cheek, wished her a Happy New Year, told her with seeming sincerity that he hoped Zachary would make it back alive, then he left to go to his room, and both knew they would probably not see each other again. Mark was flying out the next morning.

New Year's Day. No word. As the village celebrated the holiday, Carrie wandered around the festivities looking and feeling lost. By early afternoon she had returned to her clinic to spend the long dark afternoon alone. At least in the morning she could reopen her clinic and hopefully would soon be very busy again.

Oh, Zack! her heart cried, calling his name morning and afternoon; even in her sleep she'd cry out his name and sob with grief. That they had parted as they had in Anchorage that last night, Zachary throwing her a look of such contempt—that hurt so unbearably she tried never to think of it. "Carrie, you're the woman I'm in love with, the only one, the woman I'm still determined to marry," had been his last words to her, there on the dance floor, while her frightened, frozen heart had shut him out. Oh, if only her heart would refreeze now, now that he was apparently dead, and give her some peace!

The En-Ex plane conducting the search based itself in the village, and every morning, the moment the sun climbed palely above the horizon, the pilot took off, never returning until long after dark. Each evening after closing up the clinic, after hurriedly forcing down dinner, Carrie bundled up and headed out to the airstrip, beginning her nightly vigil for the return of the plane. Each night as the plane dipped down at last and rolled down the strip, Carrie closed her eyes, praying fervently that when she next opened them she would see climbing out from the plane not only Baird Williams, the pilot, but also Zachary and Matt. Surely one of these evenings . . . She simply would not give up hope!

On the seventh of January, a week after her nightly vigil had begun, the En-Ex plane arrived early, coming into view overhead within minutes after she'd arrived at the field, and today she'd arrived earlier than usual, her day having been a slow one. As she saw the plane dip down, she felt her heart leap with hope. Surely Baird wouldn't be returning this early unless—unless . . . oh, surely today he had found some sign of the downed plane and had brought back good news!

Telling herself this *must* be so, forcing out of her thoughts the memory that Baird had told her the search was so hopeless the company was about to discontinue any further flights, Carrie broke into a run toward the airstrip, her heart beating wildly. Oh, today, today, surely today . . .

The plane rolled to a stop and she saw a man climb out. In confusion, panting for breath, she stopped running, not able to sort out her thoughts. The man was too slender for the bulky Baird, yet nowhere tall or broad enough for Zachary. Had she misread the markings on the plane? Wasn't this the En-Ex plane after all? Running forward again, Carrie focused her eyes on the side of the plane and saw that it wasn't the company plane Baird had been piloting every day, as she'd assumed it was. The letters were far too blurred, paint fading away, it couldn't be the same plane she'd watched take off that very morning. But if it wasn't that plane . . .

Oh, my God! Carrie suddenly thought, and then she saw the second man climb down from the plane, so tall, broad—Zachary! Zachary and Matt had made it back on their own, in the plane they had always flown!

Bursting into a run, Carrie flew toward the two men. When she reached them, she threw herself against the taller one with the force of a hurricane, tears streaming down her cheeks.

"Oh, Zack! You made it, you're here, you're alive! Oh, Zack!"

His arms went around her, holding her close, then she heard his laugh, and Zachary dropped his arms and drew a little away, grinning at her. A thick stubble of beard covered his chin, tired creases rimmed his eyes, his cheeks looked lined and sunken. She had never seen him look so weary and strained—nor had she ever seen a sight as beautiful as his face.

"Oh, Zack," she sobbed out, again throwing herself against him, "I was so scared, so afraid. We all thought you'd crashed. How did you ever make it back?"

"With spit, chewing gum, and prayers," Zachary answered, laughing again. Again he held her close for a moment, then backed from her, his arms coming up to hold her off. His merry, dancing eyes glanced over at his companion, and Carrie's eyes followed, smiling a welcoming hello to Matt, who smiled happily back at her. The next moment her eyes returned to Zachary's face, hungrily drinking in the sight of him.

"We did have a problem and we did go down," Zachary said, in a deep soft voice. "But as you can see, we managed to get aloft again, as you should have known we would. You didn't really think I'd depart this life without ever making you mine, did you, Carrie?"

Her eyes swimming with tears, Carrie looked directly up into Zachary's gleaming dark ones, and all she could see was the loving warmth there, the passionate caring she had never dared face and accept before.

"It's so wonderful to see you again," Zachary said in the same soft voice. "That's all I could think about when we went down, that somehow, some way, I'd make it back here to you, to claim you as the woman I love."

"Oh, Zack, darling, sweetheart, I love you too!" Carrie cried in answer, and again threw herself against him. A moment later his mouth came down hungrily, possessively, on hers, making further speech impossible. But as Carrie felt his two strong arms enfold her, as her heart soared with joy, as she gave herself up to returning the kiss as passionately as she could, she knew that no further words were needed.

Now in Paperback!

My MOTHER MY SELF
BY NANCY FRIDAY

24 weeks on the New York Times Bestseller List!

In this startling, frank and provocative study of Mother/Daughter relationships, Nancy Friday reveals the most delicate, complex relationship in every woman's life. MY MOTHER/MY SELF probes the private emotions of mothers and daughters to uncover how we become the women we are.

"I'm astonished how much I've learned about my mother and myself reading Nancy Friday's candid and moving books."—*Gael Greene*

"A landmark study. Women will find this a most important book."—*Publishers Weekly*

A Dell Book • $2.50
At your local bookstore or use this handy coupon for ordering:

Dell	**DELL BOOKS**	My Mother/My Self $2.50 (15663-7)
	P.O. BOX 1000, PINEBROOK, N.J. 07058	

Please send me the above title. I am enclosing $_____
(please add 35¢ per copy to cover postage and handling). Send check or money order—no cash or C.O.D.'s. Please allow up to 8 weeks for shipment.

Mr/Mrs/Miss_____

Address_____

City_____ State/Zip_____

THE TAMING

Aleen Malcolm

Cameron—daring, impetuous girl/woman who has never known a life beyond the windswept wilds of the Scottish countryside

Alex Sinclair—high-born and quick-tempered, finds more than passion in the heart of his headstrong ward Cameron.

Torn between her passion for freedom and her long-denied love for Alex, Cameron is thrust into the dazzling social whirl of 18th century Edinburgh and comes to know the fulfillment of deep and dauntless love

A Dell Book $2.50

At your local bookstore or use this handy coupon for ordering:

Dell | **DELL BOOKS** THE TAMING $2.50 (18510-6)
P.O. BOX 1000, PINEBROOK, N.J. 07058

Please send me the above title. I am enclosing $_____
(please add 35¢ per copy to cover postage and handling). Send check or money order—no cash or C.O.D.'s. Please allow up to 8 weeks for shipment.

Mr/Mrs/Miss_____

Address_____

City_____ State/Zip_____

Bonfire

by Charles Dennis

Alan Farrel was a runaway at age 12, an ex-con at 15, a drifter, a boxer and a man no woman could refuse. Tough, charismatic, he rose from the teeming slums of New York to Hollywood's starry heights. His life was the dream-stuff movies are made of and his Polly was the only woman who lived life as lustfully as he. She loved him and had the power to destroy him!

A Dell Book $2.25

At your local bookstore or use this handy coupon for ordering:

Dell

DELL BOOKS BONFIRE (10659-1) $2.25
P.O. BOX 1000, PINEBROOK, N.J. 07058

Please send me the above title. I am enclosing $_____
(please add 35¢ per copy to cover postage and handling). Send check or money order—no cash or C.O.D.'s. Please allow up to 8 weeks for shipment.

Mr/Mrs/Miss_____

Address_____

City_____ State/Zip_____

THE DARK HORSEMAN

Marianne Harvey

Beautiful Donna Penroze had sworn to her dying father that she would save her sole legacy, the crumbling tin mines and the ancient, desolate estate *Trencobban* But the mines were failing, and Donna had no one to turn to. No one except the mysterious Nicholas Trevarvas—rich, arrogant, commanding. Donna would do anything but surrender her pride, anything but admit her irresistible longing for *The Dark Horseman*

A Dell Book $2.50

At your local bookstore or use this handy coupon for ordering:

Dell	DELL BOOKS	THE DARK HORSEMAN (11758-5) $2.50
	P.O. BOX 1000, PINEBROOK, N.J. 07058	

Please send me the above title. I am enclosing $_____
(please add 35¢ per copy to cover postage and handling). Send check or money order—no cash or C.O.D.'s. Please allow up to 8 weeks for shipment.

Mr/Mrs/Miss_____

Address_____

City_____ State/Zip_____

Dell Bestsellers

- [ ] **WHISTLE** by James Jones $2.75 (19262-5)
- [ ] **GREEN ICE** by Gerald A. Browne $2.50 (13224-X)
- [ ] **A STRANGER IS WATCHING** by Mary Higgins Clark $2.50 (18125-9)
- [ ] **AFTER THE WIND** by Eileen Lottman $2.50 (18138-0)
- [ ] **THE ROUNDTREE WOMEN · BOOK 1** by Margaret Lewerth $2.50 (17594-1)
- [ ] **THE MEMORY OF EVA RYKER** by Donald A. Stanwood $2.50 (15550-9)
- [ ] **BLIZZARD** by George Stone $2.25 (11080-7)
- [ ] **THE BLACK MARBLE** by Joseph Wambaugh $2.50 (10647-8)
- [ ] **MY MOTHER/MY SELF** by Nancy Friday $2.50 (15663-7)
- [ ] **SEASON OF PASSION** by Danielle Steel $2.25 (17703-0)
- [ ] **THE DARK HORSEMAN** by Marianne Harvey $2.50 (11758-5)
- [ ] **BONFIRE** by Charles Dennis $2.25 (10659-1)
- [ ] **THE IMMIGRANTS** by Howard Fast $2.75 (14175-3)
- [ ] **THE ENDS OF POWER** by H.R. Haldeman with Joseph DiMona $2.75 (12239-2)
- [ ] **GOING AFTER CACCIATO** by Tim O'Brien $2.25 (12966-4)
- [ ] **SLAPSTICK** by Kurt Vonnegut $2.25 (18009-0)
- [ ] **THE FAR SIDE OF DESTINY** by Dore Mullen $2.25 (12645-2)
- [ ] **LOOK AWAY, BEULAH LAND** by Lonnie Coleman $2.50 (14642-9)
- [ ] **STRANGERS** by Michael de Guzman $2.25 (17952-1)
- [ ] **EARTH HAS BEEN FOUND** by D.F. Jones $2.25 (12217-1)

At your local bookstore or use this handy coupon for ordering:

Dell **DELL BOOKS**
P.O. BOX 1000, PINEBROOK, N.J. 07058

Please send me the books I have checked above I am enclosing $_____
(please add 35¢ per copy to cover postage and handling). Send check or money order—no cash or C.O.D.'s Please allow up to 8 weeks for shipment

Mr/Mrs/Miss_____

Address_____

City_____ State/Zip_____